Choosing Peace

In His Choosing
Book 3

By

Ronna M. Bacon

John 16:33 These things I have spoken to you, that in Me you may have peace. In the world you will have tribulation; but be of good cheer, I have overcome the world.

John 14:27 Peace I leave with you, My peace I give to you; not as the world gives do I give to you. Let not your heart be troubled, neither let it be afraid.

NKJV

Table of Contents

Chapter 1
Chapter 2
Chapter 3
Chapter 4
Chapter 5
Chapter 6
Chapter 7
Chapter 8
Chapter 9
Chapter 10
Chapter 11
Chapter 12
Chapter 13
Chapter 14
Chapter 15
Chapter 16
Chapter 17
Chapter 18
Chapter 19
Chapter 20
Chapter 21
Chapter 22
Chapter 23
Chapter 24
Chapter 25
Chapter 26
Chapter 27
Chapter 28
Chapter 29
Chapter 30
Chapter 31

Chapter 32
Chapter 33
Chapter 34
Chapter 35
Chapter 36
Chapter 37
Chapter 38
Chapter 39
Epilogue
Dear Readers

The sounds of an early spring morning wafted through the air, the awakening birds and insects filling the area around them with music and noise. The scents of awakening greenery spread through the air, filling the senses of the tall man standing with his feet planted on the shore of a stream. The music of the stream echoed quietly in the air as the water tumbled over rocks and sticks and other debris, the frogs' voices loud in the early morning air.

Nickol Oakes stood, his head tilted as he listened to the sounds of God's handiwork around him, a smile lighting up his already-tanned face. His deep green eyes closed for a moment as he breathed out a prayer to his Abba Father, just thanking Him for another day to be out in nature and worship Him that way. A hand was raised to remove the cap from his dark brown hair before he settled it once more.

Looking around, Nickol smile turned to a frown. He could feel someone out there, someone watching him. He didn't have any enemies. At least, he didn't think that he did but with his line of work, it was entirely possible. He was a wildlife officer, working to protect all the animals and birds and other creatures that roamed the woods near his home town.

Nickol turned slightly. He had been asked by his boss to meet a photographer that morning, to assist with wildlife photos. Of all the men and women in the office, Nickol knew the woods the best. He had wandered them consistently as a child and teen and even on his time off, he could be found hiking the trails that wound through them, either alone or with his brother, Nigel, or with friends.

Soft footsteps caught his attention, and he turned, a frown momentarily crossing his face. If that was the photographer approaching, it could not be a man, he decided. The footsteps were too soft for that. A smile lit his face as he saw the photographer step into view.

"Nevina Bradley! I didn't know it was you I was to meet." Nickol reached to hug the lady who had stopped in front of him.

"Nickol? I didn't know that you were the worker I was to meet." Nevina shook a slim forefinger at him. "Your boss set us up." She laughed up at the tall, handsome man standing in front of her, a friend since their toddler days.

"He did. He did at that." Nicol looked around, suddenly uncomfortable and feeling danger approaching them. "What photos are you needing to get?"

Nevina shrugged for a moment, glancing around the area, her hands tightening on the straps of her backpack.

"I need to find some smaller animals and insects. My client has specific needs for their website." Nevina sighed. "And suddenly, I don't feel comfortable out here doing just that."

"I know what you mean. There's someone out here." Nickol's head was bowed as he began to pray, asking God to protect them and bring them peace in their day.

Nevina looked around once more before she stopped turning, her eyes on her friend. Her clear gray eyes studied Nickol, seeing the character of her friend, something that she appreciated from him. He had been her protector over the years, stepping into the life when he needed to and just supporting her decisions. Little did Nevina realize just how much she depended on Nickol and that he was worming his way into the depths of her heart, the very image of a knight of yore that her mother had woven into her bedtime stories.

"Where do you suggest we start?" Nevina spoke at last, bringing Nickol's eyes back to her. She pulled at the red curls of the pony tail that held the hair from her face.

"We could start here but I would suggest that we move out a ways. There are some beavers nearby and I know where a fox and her kits are. Would that work?"

"It will. He wanted fox kits but I told him that I didn't know if I could find them." Nevina sighed. "He wasn't all that specific, you know. He's like that." She didn't name the client but he was well known for his life-like nature carvings. She figured Nickol had determined who it was but she would not confirm it, not and compromise a client's confidentiality. That was important to Nevina.

"Okay, then let's head this way." Nickol took one more look around before he led the way away from the stream and deeper into the forest. He turned frequently to watch behind him, sensing that they were not alone and that someone was tracking him. Nevina had been uneasy as well, her glances behind them frequent as well.

Three hours later, Nevina found a seat on a fallen tree trunk, scrolling through the images on her camera. She was happy with what she had taken, knowing that her client would have what he wanted and needed. Her face tilted up to the sun, finding the warmth from it that she needed. A hand on her arm brought Nevina's attention to the bottle of water in Nickol's hand.

"Did you get what you wanted?" Nickol's attention was on the area around them.

"I did. He'll be happy, I know." Nevina took a swig of water and then recapped the bottle, tucking it into her backpack.

"I'm glad. Now, what do we do? I was told to work with the photographer and then take the rest of the day if we didn't need all the time." Nickol watched his friend closely, seeing subtle changes in her face that had not been there the week before. "Nevina? What's going on? You're scared."

"I am, Nickol, and I don't know why. Someone has been around my home and around the studio out back. I talked with John but there's no evidence that he can find." John was a police detective and friend of theirs. "Peter has been around, tightening up the security that he can." Peter, a cousin of John's, had a security team and alway took care of their friends.

"That's good but it still doesn't make it easier for you." Nickol was on his feet, a hand reaching for his backpack and then Nevina's hand. "We need to move, Nevina."

Nevina was on her feet, moving rapidly away from the area with Nickol. Something had spooked him, she decided, but just what that was? She didn't know. A sound echoed around them before Nevina was grabbing at her shoulder, blood spouting from between her fingers. She stumbled, her hand torn from Nickol's. A whimper sounded from her quietly before she was tumbling down the low hill, her head thudding against another fallen tree before she was still, not moving. This left Nickol staring in horror at her before he was sliding down the hill to reach for her.

Horror covered his face as he saw the blood on her shoulder. He desperately ripped into his backpack for his first aid kit, the packaging from the bandage shoved back into it. The bandage was shoved at the wound as he tried his best to stop the bleeding. This was not good, Nickol decided. There was no cell service in this particular area of the woods and it would be a long trek back to the parking lot.

On his feet, Nickol had both backpacks on his shoulders before he gently gathered Nevina into his arms. He knew of a small one-room cabin not that far from there where he could find shelter for his friend and take better care of her.

—

11

Stepping carefully, Nickol walked towards the cabin, his attention divided between watching his path and the lady in his arms. Nevina had not moved or roused since she fell. He was worried about her, not knowing how deep the wound was and if it had hit anything vital. A hand reached for the cabin door as he approached it, shoving it open.

Nickol hesitated for a moment before he stepped into the cabin, the musty, slightly damp smelling air hitting his nostrils. He held back the sneeze that started before he was heading for the rickety couch, laying Nevina down. He still for a moment, a hand on her hair before he struggled out of their backpacks and dropped them to the floor.

Heading for the outdoors, Nickol grabbed at the axe by the door. He needed kindling to start the fire and also wood to feed it. Back inside, Nickol carefully laid a fire, praying that the chimney was clear. Nevina needed shelter at least for the time being and until he could think of a way to get her back to a vehicle and then to medical aid.

Turning back to his pack, Nickol pulled out the emergency blankets, laying one out flat in front of the fire. He stood for a moment, debating with himself before he reached to gather Nevina close to him once more and then gently place her on the blanket, another one tucked around her. Nickol hesitated for a moment before he reached into the backpack once more, retrieving his first aid kit. Scissors in hand, his head bowed as he prayed for his friend. He would need to carefully cut away her jacket and sweatshirt to assess the damage that had been done to her. He had no doubt that she had been shot but he had not hear the shot. That scared him.

Thirty minutes later, Nickol sat back. He had managed to clean the wound as best as he could with his limited resources and bandage it. He just needed to get her out of there. Darkness was already falling and it would be too dangerous for him to even attempt the walk out that night. He would need to wait for morning.

A sound at the door early the next morning had Nickol raising his head. He had taken a position near the fireplace where he could monitor Nevina and also maintain the fire. He frowned. That sounded like a person, he decided, as he rose to his feet and headed that way. Nickol came to an abrupt halt as the door swung open on creaky hinges and three men appeared, weapons pointed at him. He froze, waiting for someone to speak.

None of the men spoke. One walked over and not so gently kicked at Nevina, the only sound from her a groan at the viciousness of the kick. She didn't rouse at all.

Nickol spun, ready to take on the man, his mouth open to speak. But he could no further in his actions of words. A heavy blow from a revolver butt struck Nickol's head and he collapsed to the floor, to lie in a crumpled heap. The three men stared down at the two before they walked away, the fire extinguished. Their thoughts were that the two would not survive to make it back to safety.

Nickol roused slowly, a hand going to the back of his head. He raised his head slightly, staring around through blurry eyes. No, he decided, it was not his home. He just didn't know where he was. His eyes lighting on a still form, Nickol struggled to his hands and knees and crawled towards the pile of blankets. A hand went out to touch the form, surprise on his face as he realized it was Nevina. How they had gotten to that cabin, he just couldn't remember but both of them were hurt. And it would be up to him to somehow get them to safety. He collapsed once more, an arm around his friend, seeking to keep her warm. Nickol just didn't have it in him at that point to struggle to the fireplace and relight the fire.

It was early the next morning before Nickol roused once more. A hand on his face had brought him out of his stupor. Opening his eyes, he looked around, finding that Nevina had roused as well and turned to him, a hand on his cheek bringing his attention to her.

"Nickol?" Nevina's voice was low and hoarse. "What happened? Why do I hurt?"

"You were shot, Nevina, yesterday I think it was. Some men found us and knocked me out." Nickol managed to struggle to sit upright, reaching for his backpack and the bottles of water. He twisted off the cap from one and helped Nevina to drink. "I need to get you out of here. You're running a fever. I can't treat your wound." Nickol was almost in tears at that thought, a man who rarely allowed his emotions to get to that point. But this was his best friend who was hurt.

"I can walk." Nevina tried to push herself up and collapsed back in pain. "But then again, maybe I can't." Her eyes closed as she slipped away from Nickol.

Nickol was on his feet, staggering as he did so. He was out of the cabin, searching for the men, his eyes blurring at times as he struggled to stay upright. Back in the cabin, Nickol stood, staring down at Nevina. He had to get them out of there and do it that day. Something was sending him away from the cabin. He had learned early to listen to his instincts. Quickly packing away what he had taken from the backpacks, he shouldered them. Nickol hesitated for a moment, knowing that it would hurt him to bend over and gather Nevina up but he had to do it. His head raised for a moment as he looked up, begging God for the strength that he needed right then.

Walking away from the cabin, Nickol's steps were slow and hesitant at times. He carefully set each foot down before lifting the other one. He had to. If he tried to walk with his normal stride, he would be on the ground and who knew if he would ever be able to upright himself again. Nevina needed him to stay on his feet.

The air was damp with a chill wind blowing. Nickol shivered as he felt it, his arms tightening around Nevina in an attempt to keep her warm. The walk that should have taken just a few hours stretched out in the early evening. Nickol had prayed that he would make it to safety and a vehicle before dark. That wasn't happening. Instead, he began to search for somewhere that was sheltered and where he could build a small fire to offset the night coldness. Finding a small cave-like opening, Nickol headed that way, gently setting Nevina down until he could once more set out the emergency blankets. He started a small fire, careful with where it was set, gathering wood and sticks and branches to help him feed it overnight.

Seating himself beside Nevina, Nickol could feel the fever that she was fighting as he drew her into his arms, wrapping a blanket around them. He didn't like having to do this, being very careful in how he treated any lady but he really didn't have a choice, now did he? Nickol dozed off and on over the night, awakening to replenish the fire and then to get some fluid into Nevina. She had fought him at first on this but soon she just didn't. Her throat would move as she swallowed before she turned her head into his shoulder. She just wasn't wakening.

Chapter 3

Sometime over the middle of the night, Nickol felt himself raised to his feet, an arm around him bracing him upright. He blinked at the man beside him, not sure who he was and not getting a clear look at him in the dimness. He sensed that there were others there as well. Nickol began to protest as he was led away from the cave, the fire extinguished, and the backpacks on other shoulders.

Nickol kept stopping and turning, trying to find his way back to Nevina.

"I need to find Nevina. She's hurt. I need to look after her." Nickol was almost in tears as he spoke, not wanting to abandon his friend.

"We have, Nickol." The voice sounded familiar to Nickol but he could not put a name to it. "She's with us. Come. Let's get you to safety and then we can treat your friend." The older man convinced Nickol's at long last that Nevina was indeed being carried out.

Nickol sank down on the truck seat, his arm out to wrap around Nevina and hold her close to him. He was aware enough to know that she was fighting a fever.

"She's sick. Nevina needs help." Nickol was almost incoherent with his words.

The three men in the truck with the couple shared a look before the older man shook his head. This was not what they had been expecting to find. They had been sent out to look for Nickol when word had reached them that he was missing. None of them had expected to find him injured or to find Nevina as sick as she was. She had not been reported missing to them and that concerned them.

Later that morning, Nickol's brother, Nigel, hammered at Nickol's front door, waiting for his brother to respond. When the door didn't open, Nigel paced around the house, trying to find Nickol and seeing no evidence that he had been there. Peeking through the garage window, Nigel frowned. Nickol's truck was there. Spinning, he ran for the house, fumbling as he found his key to the door and then keying in his security password. He searched the sprawling one-level house and didn't see any evidence that Nickol had been there for days. Nigel was back out of the house, his phone out to place a call. He slid to a halt as he saw John, a police detective friend, approaching.

"John? What are you doing there?" Nigel was puzzled at how John knew to appear.

"Nickol's boss called. He didn't call him when he was supposed to and hasn't been in the office for three days. He wanted a welfare check." John looked past Nigel. "You've been inside?"

"I have. His truck is in the garage but he's not here. It doesn't look as if he has been in a few days. I don't like this, John." Nigel's face grew dark with his worry.

"Nor do I. Okay. So, where would he be?" John sighed as his phone vibrated, pulling it out to read a text message. "Nigel? Nickol's friends with Nevina, correct?"

Nigel stared at him for a moment, not quite comprehending why he was being asked a question, the answer to which was obvious.

"He is. He calls her his best friend. They have been friends since toddlers. Why?" Nigel's face paled. "Is she missing to?"

"She is. Apparently, she was to meet with Nigel who would take her to do some of her photos. His boss arranged that. She hasn't been heard from either. Jerome is doing a welfare check for her." John paced around the house and then through it, seeing it was as Nigel had commented. Nickol had not been here. He peered down at his phone again, noting his message from Jerome. "Her car is at her home but she's not. We'll need to find her family to search her home."

Nigel shook his head.

"I have a key to her home. Both Nickol and I do. Her parents are away a lot and she wanted someone here that would be available if she needed them." Nigel ran for his car, not waiting for John to follow. He had already locked up Nickol's house and had been waiting for John to respond with what they would do or search next.

John watched his drive away before he shook his head. Nigel shouldn't have done that, but he did. He drove off after him, a message sent to Jerome as to what was happening. John worried about his friend, not knowing where he was. All he could do was pray for him and that he as not going to have an adventure as their friends Slavin and Roane had had.

John paced through Nevina's home, watching as Nigel did as well.

"Nigel? What are your thoughts?" John stood in the hallway, staring back into the living room.

"It's as she leaves it in the morning. She likes to leave it tidy for when she comes home. She doesn't want to face a mess as she puts it when she's tired." Nigel was frustrated. He had prayed that there would be some sort of sign of trouble in either Nickol's or Nevina's homes. And that had not happened.

"Okay. So this doesn't help us find them. I need to head for another crime scene. Call me if you hear from either one." John walked away, his gaze searching the area but not seeing anyone who stood out.

Nigel locked up the house, turning from it with worry in his heart. Where was his brother and their friend? He drove away, heading back to his brother's home, in the hope that he had shown up.

Two days later, Nigel once more approached his brother's home, frowning as he saw a truck backing out of the driveway. It was Nickol's truck. He followed it as it drove off, not certain where Nickol would be headed. Following it to a local motel on the other side of town, Nigel parked and turned off his truck, a hand on the door handle to be ready to jump from his truck and then head for Nickol. He paused. It wasn't Nickol who jumped from the truck and then ran from sight. He didn't know the man. Nigel's gaze went back to the truck, a frown deeper on his face. What had just happened? He reached for his phone to call John, not sure if it was a situation that John needed to become involved in but seeing as Nickol was a missing person, the authorities did need to know.

John approached Nigel where he stood leaning against his truck, his eyes not moving from his brother's truck, barely glancing at John.

"Nigel? Any sign of them?" John sighed as Nigel shook his head.

"I don't know if he's in there or not. It was just so strange." Nickol frowned once more as he watched the motel room door open and a man emerge, heading for the truck and then driving off. "That's not Nickol."

"No, it's not." John's phone was out to have the truck stopped even as he walked rapidly across to the room and tapped at the still open door. The room was empty and didn't even seem to have been used. "This is strange, Lord. Where is my friend?"

Chapter 4

Walking back towards Nigel, John was definitely puzzled and also frustrated. The crime scene techs had gone through the room. Video surveillance had been obtained from the office as had the registration card. It was not Nickol who had been in the room. They still had no idea of where he was or who had taken his truck to use. That was something John needed to determine and he wasn't sure if he would even be able to.

"John?" Nigel's voice had John raising his head, shaking it at his friend. Nigel's eyes closed. They were no closer to finding his brother and Nevina. How did they do that? "What now?"

"What now? We continue to investigate. I have a team heading out to the woods where he was to meet Nevina and searching there. We'll continue to watch for him. At the moment, Nigel, we don't know where he is or why he is hiding if that is what he is doing."

"What you're not saying is that he could be hidden somewhere and in grave danger." Nigel didn't express his worse fears, that Nickol was dead and that they would never find his body.

"About that." John walked away at last, at a loss to know what to do next. Jerome had been around, their discussion deep and dark but one that held no clues for where to search next.

The next morning, Nigel once more headed for his brother's home on his way to work. He frowned as he slowly drove by. Something seemed different but he couldn't stop, not at that time. He would be back that afternoon and searching, he knew.

That afternoon, Nigel fitted his key into the lock on the steel front door and unlocked it, stepping inside. Something was different he knew. A glance at the security system showed that it was off, something that only happened when Nickol was home. Nigel toed off his shoes and then walked through to the kitchen, stopping in shock as he saw his brother standing at the counter, his hands flat on the countertop, his head hanging down as he waited for the coffee to perk.

"Nickol?" Nigel walked to stand beside him, his head tilted to study his brother. "You look rough. Where have you been?" He waited patiently for Nickol to look up, shocked at the devastation, shame, and worry that showed in his brother's eyes. "Nickol?"

"Nigel? You're here? Of course, you are. Let me get the coffees and then we'll talk. This involves someone else." Nickol turned his attention back to the mugs, reaching for a third one. This act puzzled Nigel before he reached for his brother's hand, stopping the motion of it.

"Nickol? What's this?" Nigel pointed to the ring on his brother's left hand. "You're not dating anyone. Why are you wearing a wedding band?"

Nickol drew in a deep breath. He had tried to avoid this but he couldn't. He didn't hear the door opening behind him and his parents and John appearing just in time to hear Nigel's question, sending their eyes to search one another before their attention went back to Nickol.

"I can explain, Nigel. But it involves Nevina as well." Nickol turned, momentarily startled at the sight of the three standing behind him before he brushed past them, heading for the living room and to where Nevina had curled up on the couch, wrapped in a blanket. He sat, just reaching to wrap her close to him.

Nevina roused slightly and then turned her face into Nickol's shoulder, sleeping once more. The wound that had gone untreated had become infected. Even though she was on treatment for it now, she still slept from the pain and the fever that had wracked her body.

His family followed, his brother with the tray of mugs filled with coffee. John frowned at Nickol for a moment before he sat, his eyes flickering between the couple.

"Just one question, Nickol. Have you given statements?" John didn't want them speaking to anyone if they had not.

"We have. The officer who brought us home made sure of that. He said he'd reach out tomorrow to you or Jerome." Nickol's head went down for a moment. His strength was still not back to what it had been and he struggled at times with headaches.

"Okay. I'll watch for that." John shared a look with Nigel before looking over at Niall.

—

"Son, let's pray for you and then you can explain what is going on." Niall simply bowed his head and prayed for his son and the lady who now seemed to be part of his life. Nevina had always been welcomed to their home and family. It now seemed as if she was a permanent part of it.

Raising their heads, the group gathered in the living room kept their attention on the couple in front of them. Nickol's attention was on Nevina, who still slept, her hand now tight in his. Nickol sighed. He had no way to know how to explain what had happened. He prayed for the words to explain at the same time as he prayed for protection for the lady who was now a more important part of his life. He had had to admit over the last couple of days that he had been in loved with this lady for years but had not wanted to destroy their friendship by stating that to her. He had no idea of how she felt. Nevina could keep her feelings hidden at times.

"Son?" Niall's voice brought his son's gaze to him. "Tell us what happened. It's okay if it's not in order and you leave out things. We'll talk about it more than once. For now, just give the highlights if that's all you can do." He watched with compassion as Nickol's eyes closed as he struggled with his emotions.

"I can, Dad. It's not pretty, some of it. And I wish that it had never happened but it did." Nickol could hardly speak for the way that his emotions were affecting him. He felt his father's ar;m around him as Niall moved to sit beside him. "How do I start, Dad? How do I tell you what happened when I don't really remember that much? It's like it's a movie that wasn't clear and I missed parts of it."

"Just talk to us, son. Tell us what you can. Nigel and John will take notes, if that helps." He had watched the two younger men retrieve pads of paper and pens. "Then, we'll go back over it and sort it out. God is here with you, son, with you and Nevina. He is protecting you. Part of that protection is sometimes not letting you remember. And He will aid you in finding the peace that you both will need in this situation. He has promised that, son. Never doubt His promises. They never fail."

Nickol had turned to his father, his eyes closing as he struggled with his tears. He was not a crying man but the trauma of the last few days had driven him to that point. His arm tightened around his bride even as Niall's arm tightened around his son's shoulder. This was one time that neither Niall or Ami could make better for their son. All they could do was pray for the couple and then walk beside them over the next weeks or however long it took for the investigation to prove who had wanted to harm either or both of the couple.

—

Chapter 5

Nickol's eyes dropped to Nevina, seeing the pain and stress that still lined her face. He had tried too hard, God help him, to protect her and get her to safety. Someone had stepped in and helped them.

His mind tracked back to when he had awakened in the house, a soft bed underneath his body and warm covers over him. He had frowned and then shoved at the blankets, finding clean clothes waiting for him. Dressing rapidly, Nickol had staggered for a moment, the sharp pain from the head wound stopping him in his tracks. He shook it off as best as he could, determined to find Nevina.

Searching what seemed to be an empty house, Nickol had paused at a doorway, shooting a glance behind him before he slowly approached the bed to drop to his knees. His hand reached for Nevina's, his other hand on her cheek. She had been treated, he assumed, for her wound. Just who had found them? That was a question he needed an answer to but so far, no one had appeared who could answer that.

Nevina shifted slightly as she sensed someone near her. Her eyes opened slightly as she squinted in the early afternoon light.

"Nickol? Is that you?" Her voice was barely audible.

—

"It is, sweetheart. How are you feeling?" Nickol groaned for a moment. That was such a mundane way to start a conversation.

"Okay, I guess. What day is it?" Nevina frowned at him as he shook his head. "You don't know?"

"No, I don't. I was hoping that you did. Guess not." Nickol helped her to sit up and then to stand. "There's no one here. And I don't know where here is." His arm wrapped around her to lead her from the bedroom and towards the living room. Seating her, he crouched down beside her, his arm still around her. He was deeply worried about her. "You scared me."

"I did? I'm sorry but I don't understand why." She felt at her shoulder. "What did I do?" Nevina looked around before she looked at him, seeing the ravages of what he had gone through on his face. "Nickol? What all happened?"

"You were shot. I had managed to get us to shelter in that little cabin. Sometime that first night some men appeared. They knocked me out. Over the next day or so, I think, I managed to look after you, getting you on your feet when I needed to. Then some other men appeared." Nickol frowned at her as something tickled at the edge of his memory, something that he could not quite remember. "I think I know them. I just don't know who."

"That's okay. So, we're not in that cabin any more." Nevina didn't look away from him. "But something did happen. I vaguely remember them being here."

"They were." Sorrow and despair settled on Nickol's face. "We're married, Nevina. We didn't have a choice, I don't think. They just told us that we would marry. Neither one of us was in any shape to say no." His head bent as his emotions got the better of him.

Nevina stared at him in shock and then stared at her hand. It did indeed have a wedding band on it. She drew in a deep breath. What she did next was so crucial to how they continued. Lord, I know that you have allowed this. Please, Lord, let me have the right words to say. I don't want to lose my best friend, my hero, my knight in shining armour who has stood beside me for so many years. Let us find Your peace in all this, no matter what happens next.

"How did they get us to agree? I really don't remember much." Nevina rested her hand on Nickol's cheek, feeling the wetness from his tears, sparking her own in response.

"I'm not sure. I don't remember much other than they told us that we had to marry. They took me with them to get the license and then the bands. I chose them. This is the one that I would have chosen for you at some point." Nickol didn't hear his words, didn't hear himself putting his feelings for her out there but Nevina did and treasured them in her heart. "I know they had a minister but he wasn't from our town." Nickol was on his feet, heading for the kitchen, finding bottles of water and then returning to sit beside her. "I'm sorry, Nevina. This is not how you should have married."

"It's okay, Nickol. It's okay. God allowed it, didn't He?" At his nod, her head went down on his shoulder. "Now, we need to determine where we are and get us out of here."

"We will. For now, let's spend some time in prayer." Nickol's head was bent as he crumpled inside, his heart breaking for Nevina, and as he begged his Abba Father for peace in their situation.

Nevina stared at him before she was on her feet, not as steady as she would have liked to be. Their backpacks sat by the door. She reached for hers, turning to find Nickol there to take it from her.

"We need to leave, Nickol. I don't feel safe here. Can we do that?" Nevina felt as if she was begging him to walk away from that house. Something was driving her to leave, whether or not he went with her.

"We can, Nevina. We just need to watch how much you do." Nickol reached for hers hand, the backpacks over his shoulders as he opened the door and then walked away from the house, his steps measured and slow to match hers. His head was in constant motion as he studied the area around them, not feeling as safe as he thought they should be.

They were both surprised to find that they were in their own town. Nickol paused to stare back at the house, memorizing the number and street. He frowned. He didn't know the owners but he would each out to John. Somehow, they had appeared in their town once more. Nickol could vaguely remember speaking with an officer. Only he didn't think that officer was from this town.

—

30

"Nevina? We were moved here at some point and I don't remember that. We were in another town." Nickol tugged her forward, heading for a diner that he could see just up the road from them. "I know that we gave statements. I'm just not sure what town that was in."

"I do remember, sort of." Nevina groaned as he grinned down at her. "That didn't make a lot of sense. Can we rest somewhere, Nickol? I don't know if I can walk any further."

"Here, have a seat on this bench. I'm going in and grabbing us something to eat and something to hot to drink. Then, we'll find a taxi to get us home." Nickol's eyes closed. "Which home do we go to?"

"Go to yours. I need to get some clothes." Nevina's voice was sober as she spoke. She knew without asking that they had to stay together. It was not what she wanted. She only wanted to curl up in her own bed, the doors locked behind her. That wouldn't happen now.

"We can stop on our way there." Nickol looked up as he heard his name called. "Here's Tony. Tony?"

"Nickol? You're back but you look rough." Tony, a mutual friend, looked past him at Nevina. "Nevina?"

"Tony, can you take us to my home so I can grab some stuff and then take us to Nickol's?" Nevina was on her feet, swaying even as Nickol wrapped an arm around her.

—

"I can do that." Tony was puzzled. He ran a nearby hardware store and had been out on a delivery when he spotted them. "I won't ask but you do have a story to tell me at some point."

"We will, Tony. First, we need to find our families and then John or Jerome." Nickol slid in beside Nevina, his hand reaching for hers. "It's been a long few days. And we were both injured."

Tony watched as Nickol unlocked his house door and then disappeared inside after Nevina. He felt danger encroaching around them and could only pray for his friend and his lady.

Chapter 6

Nickol came back to the present, his head and shoulders still bent with the weight of what he was carrying in worry and fear. This was something outside of what he normally tackled. And he still had to speak with his employer. That was a conversation that was slated for the next day. His arm tightened around Nevina who still slept.

Niall's arm tightened even more around his son before he again prayed audibly for Nickol and Nevina. There were many unanswered questions. Speculation in his mind was rife as he was sure it was with the others.

"Nevina's parents? Can we reach them?" Ami studied her son, Nigel's arm around his mother.

"I don't know. She wasn't sure where they were at present. John?" :Nickol looked up, squinting against the headache that had begun to rage.

"I can do that. I think Jerome was on the hunt for them and may even had contacted them." John didn't give away much of the investigation. He couldn't. "Do you remember at all anything about the men?"

"No, I don't. I didn't get that good a look at them. And the house address is written on that piece of paper there beside you." Nickol shared a look with John who had reached for the paper and read the address. John shook his head slightly, letting Nickol know that they would talk further.

"I think we need to let you two rest, son." Niall was on his feet, allowing Nickol to rise and gather Nevina into his arms.

The family watched as Nickol walked slowly away from them. They heard soft movement before a door closed and Nickol was back with them.

"What can we do for you, bro?" Nigel stood beside his brother, a hand on his arm keeping him upright. "You need to sleep. And to take something for that headache."

"I know, Nige. I know but I want to solve this." Nickol was becoming stubborn, something that happened when he wasn't well.

"Not tonight, Nickol. Tonight, you sleep and try to recover. This has been traumatic for both of you and you both need to heal." Ami was adamant that her son found his rest. "Go on with Nigel. We'll stay the night, just in case you need us." Ami didn't continue. She was afraid that one or the other or both of the young couple would disappear on them once more and never be found.

Nickol finally nodded, his eyes closing against the pain from his headache. He allowed Nigel to turn him back towards his bedroom. He refused to change into his night clothes, instead just dropping to the top of the covers. Nigel found a blanket to cover his brother, a hand resting on Nickol's shoulder as he prayed for him. They were in uncharted waters, he decided, and would need to bring in everyone that they could to investigate. There was no way that their friends would stay out of that investigation.

Niall looked around as he heard Nigel approaching the kitchen. John had left, disturbed by what he had been told. He headed for the office, determined to track down whatever town it was that Nickol and Nevina had been held in and also to verify if the marriage really was registered and legitimate.

"He's asleep?"

"He is, Dad. I don't get it. Who does this?" Nigel was worried for his brother and for Nevina. He had no idea what lay ahead of them. He was just so afraid that he would lose his brother to death.

"I don't know, son. Mom reached out to Emma and asked for her help. She's away at the moment but promised to have someone start a search." Niall's hand on his son's shoulder had him sitting down at the table. "We need to eat something, even just a sandwich. You need to work tomorrow?"

"I do, Dad, but I can work from here, I think. Jack's okay with that, he told me when I spoke with him earlier." Nigel worked as a copywriter and editor for a local magazine.

"That's good. Mom and I have appointments in the afternoon. We'll see what we can accomplish before then." Niall sat as well, his head bowing to pray over their meal but also to petition God for a quick resolution to whatever it was that Nickol had become involved in.

"Slavin called me earlier, just before we had that conversation with Nickol. He wants to meet with them but won't push it right now." Slavin and his now wife, Shaye, had had an adventure as it was termed as had other friends, Roane and Ragen. "Slavin and Roane will be good to talk with them."

"They will be." Niall sat, his sandwich held in his hand, as he pondered what Nickol had said. It didn't make any sense, he decided. They were missing something and he had no idea what that something was.

Awakening in the night, Nickol's head raised slightly from his pillow. He listened to the faint sounds of a whimper and then was on his feet, searching for the source of it. He stood beside Nevina's bed before he had dropped to his knees beside it, his arm around her.

"Nevina? Nevina?" Nickol kept his voice low, even as he watched her eyes flicker open.

"Nickol? What time is it? And just where are we? Are we safe?" Nevina shoved at him before she sat up, her feet hitting the wood floor.

"We're safe, sweetheart. We're at my home." Nickol moved to sit beside her. "How are you feeling?" He watched her closely as she felt at her shoulder and then shrugged.

"Okay, I guess. The wound is healing, I suppose. We'll need to find someone to look at it." Nevina leaned against him, a yawn cracking across her face. "I'm tired, Nickol. When will this be over? And who is behind this?" Her eyes closed as she slept once more, not seeing the tender look that appeared on Nickol's face.

"Soon, I pray, sweetheart. I want to go on with a life with you. And I don't know if you'll stay with me." Nickol wrapped an arm around her before he swung her up into his arms and headed for his recliner in the living room. Sitting, he just cuddled Nevina close to him, not even thinking of a blanket to cover them. His head went back as he too slept, the last few days almost more than he could handle.

Ami had roused as she heard the soft voices and then had risen as well, following her son to the living room. She shook her head before she reached for the blanket on the couch, tucking it around the couple. Her hands rested on their heads as she prayed for them, knowing that whatever they were facing was far from over and would only get more dangerous for them.

Chapter 7

Rousing later that morning, Nickol's head raised slightly as he squinted around the room. He didn't remember moving to the living room during the night and wondered at that. He looked down at Nevina, a frown on his face as she still slept. When had this happened, he wondered? Nickol could hear the faint sounds of movement in the kitchen and soft conversation.

A sound to his left had his head whipping around that way. John sat there, working away on his laptop.

"John? What are you doing here? Aren't you supposed to be on a crime scene somewhere?" Nickol had to clear his throat to speak.

John looked up, a smile on his face. He had been told to find Nickol and talk to both him and Nevina. Jerome had been specific on that.

"I was told to find you. We need to talk, all three of us. You need to awaken Nevina." John watched as Nickol shoved away the blanket and then rose, Nevina in his arms and stalked away from the room. His mouth opened and then closed before he shook his head. Nickol was protective of his lady, John decided. Thinking back over the years, John realized that Nickol had always been like that.

Nickol gently laid Nevina back on her bed and covered her, tucking the covers tight around her neck.

—

He stooped, hesitated, and then kissed her temple before he prayed for his lady and then walked away to his own bedroom. He scrubbed at his face, decided that a shower, shave, and clean clothes took priority over whatever it was that John wanted.

A tap at his door as he sat on his bed, pulling on his socks, had him raising his head. Nigel slipped inside, just to sit beside his brother, his shoulder touching Nickol's.

"Nickol? What is going on? Do you even know?" Nigel was genuinely puzzled at what was going on. He had fielded calls from both Slavin and Roane but could give them no real answers.

"I don't know, Nige. I really done. All I know is that I was asked to help Nevina with some photos. I didn't see who shot her. It scared me, Nigel. I thought that she would die on me. And I don't know who it was that attacked me. I suspect that it was the same men but I can't prove it. I didn't see them either time. And I don't know who it was that brought us to safety and had Nevina assessed at a hospital. It was just so bizarre."

"It sounds it. I don't get it. Leaving you alone like that? They either thought you would die or that you would walk out on your own. What if you hadn't been able to? Who would have found you?"

"That I don't know. I sent Emma a   text with the address and the name of who I know lives there." Nickol looked around before he mentioned the name in a very low voice.

—

Nigel stared at his brother, shocked at who he had named before his head was nodding.

"There have always been rumours about that family." Nigel's attention was not on his brother but on the soft cream of the wall across from him and the picture of a waterfall that Nevina had enlarged and presented to Nickol for his birthday the year before. He frowned as he thought through what he knew of the family.

"I know. I wish that I hadn't gotten involved as I did, but I am. I wonder if it had been a set up, that Nevina was asked to obtain photos and that they knew I would be the one asked to help her. Everyone else in the office was busy that day. Nevina said it was specific as to the date that she was requested to do the photos."

"It was? Does John know that?" Nigel was on his feet, dragging Nickol with him towards the living room. "John? Did you know that Nevina was asked to take those photos on a specific date? Nickol just mentioned that."

John looked up from his notes, blinking for a moment as his attention came to the brothers.

"No, I don't know that we had that information. Nickol?" John pointed at a seat. "Sit, Talk to me about that."

"I don't know much other than that Nevina mentioned in passing at one point that it had been specific to that day. She didn't understand it. I think that she still has the emails but I won't awaken her to ask her for them." Nickol was digging in his heels and neither of the men with him could blame him.

"I see." John had his phone out, sending off a text to Jerome. He frowned at Jerome's response. "Somehow, Jerome has managed to find that out. Would your employer have know that?"

"I suspect that he did. I was chosen to go with her. I don't know if it was specific that I go or not." Nickol's eyes slid shut as his headache suddenly worsened. "I don't know what to say or even think any more." He sank back against the couch, his eyes closing as he too slept.

Nigel stared at him and then at John, who shrugged. John was on his feet, heading for the door. He needed to be in the office for a meeting. Talking with both Nickol and Nevina would need to wait.

Nigel paced the kitchen, his eyes turning every once and a while towards the living room. Hearing soft movement, he stepped to the doorway, finding Nevina heading his way, a hand holding her arm.

"Nevina?" Nigel gave a grin at her as she jumped.

"I didn't know that you were here. Nickol's sleeping, isn't he?" She turned that way, intending on finding him until Nigel stopped her with a hand on her arm. "Nigel?"

"Come and have something to eat. Just some soup and your coffee. Some toast." Nigel seated her and then swiftly prepared a meal for her. He sat nearby, watching as she hesitated before she lifted her spoon. "How are you feeling?"

"Sore. Tired. Worried. Scared. Wanting to find peace in all this and not doing that. How does that sound?" Nevina didn't look up at him but knew that his grin would have been growing with each word that she said.

"Sounds about right. John needs to talk to you again but he'll be back. Peter will be around as well. He wants to go over security with you." Peter was John's cousin and had a security team.

"I know that he will. And I don't have to like it, do I?" Nevina was grumpy, something not usual for her. She refused to apologize, knowing that Nigel would just shrug it off. "What do we do, Nigel? How do we stay safe? And this?" She held up her left hand. "How do we find whoever it was that made us do this?"

"Emma's looking into that for us." Emma was a friend of theirs who ran a business finding information and people that no one else could find. Her husband, Abe, also had a security team. "And I am sure that Abe is weighing in on security. He has already spoken with Peter, Richard, and Don. You know all four of them are security teams."

"I know. That scares me, Nigel." Nevina felt an arm around her as Nickol found her and sat beside her, a nod at Nigel as he rose to find food for his brother.

"It scares me too, sweetheart." Nickol couldn't put into words his exact feelings. It was too soon. He was just so afraid that he would lose Nevina.

—

Chapter 8

Two days later, Nevina stood in the office at her own home. She was saddened. She had worked hard to set it up just how she wanted it to be. Now, because of someone else who had directed something in her life that they had no business doing, she was being forced to give it up and move it all to another place. Nevina wiped at the tears on her face. She was healing physically but emotionally and mentally she was hurting and didn't know how to cope or even who to speak with. She didn't know anyone who had been in the position that she was in, forced to marry without any choice in it. Although, she had to admit to herself, she would have chosen Nickol. She had always had a crush on him.

Nickol stood where he couldn't be seen, his heart breaking for his bride. He was angry, angry that someone had taken over their lives. He spun and walked away, finding Peter waiting outside for him as well as Richard. Richard's team member, Naomi, was around, a cousin of Nevina's.

"Nickol? What can we do?" Peter's hand stopped Nickol in his tracks. "What do you need?"

"This to be over?" Nickol ran his hands through his hair. "Nevina needs to talk to someone about what happened."

"And so do you." Richard was nodding, guessing at the emotions roiling through his friend. "I know of some that this happened to. They work for the Barnabas Foundation. Barnabas reached out last night, asking what they could do. These couples have offered to speak with you. There are two that I know of. And there are others as well that we may be able to find."

"That works. When? Tomorrow is Saturday. Is that too soon?" Nickol was desperate to at least find someone to talk to.

"No, that's fine. They suggested it." Richard walked away to make that call to Barnabas to confirm the date and time.

Peter watched Richard and then turned to Nickol.

"How are you really doing, Nickol?" He waited patiently for a response.

"To tell you the truth? I don't know. I'm hurting for Nevina, for myself, for our families. I want this over. I want to know who is behind this and we don't have a sense of who that is. I heard from John that the house had been sold just in the last couple of weeks and that the person we suspected is not involved. Unfortunately, it was sold to a numbered company and he is having trouble working through the layers."

"He will. Emma likely is working on that." Peter had faith in his friend, that she would indeed do just that. "But for now? What can we do for you two?" He looked past Nickol to see Nevina approaching. "Nevina's here."

"She is?" Nickol turned, his arms reaching to hug his lady.

<hr>

Nevina clung to him, her emotions too high for her to even speak. Peter frowned at her and then was on the run into the house. Naomi was running after him, sensing that something had happened.

"Nevina? What's in the house?" Nickol waited for her to speak, his eyes on Richard as that man approached them and then shoved them into the house, the door closed behind them.

"Someone has been in here, Nickol. In my office. I can't go back in there." Nevina's fear was shuddering through her, causing to shake.

Richard's phone was out as he called in help. John shared a look with Jerome as he took the call and was on his feet, both men heading for Nevina's.

John walked back towards the outdoors, finding the officers who had been searching the yards and garage.

"What did you find?" He waited patiently for them to speak, staring at the evidence bags that they were holding up. "All that?"

"All that, John." David, the one officer who had searched the garage, shook his head. "They really wanted to keep an eye on her. Do we know when these were placed?"

"I don't know that we can find out. She doesn't have any security cameras on the exterior the house. And her security system? She hasn't been using it, hasn't for months. She didn't see a need for that." John was frustrated with Nevina and it showed for a moment as anger flickered across his face. He sighed.

What was done was done. He could not change anything about that.

"I see. She's not living here now, is she?" David looked past John to where Richard and Peter stood.

"No, she's not. She and Nickol are married and are living at his place. And I know that he has good security. He did that when Slavin faced what he did." John turned back to study the surrounding homes. "Someone is going door to door?"

"We are but we're not expecting too much. Where we found the cameras and motion sensors were sheltered."

"That's not what I wanted to hear." John turned back to the house, finding Nickol waiting for him. "Nickol?"

"Who did this? How did they get into her house and when?" Nickol had to tamp down his anger. It wasn't helping the situation, even though he felt justified in feeling that.

"I don't know, Nickol. We found no evidence of who had done this. We don't know why." John was angry as well and stalked past his friend on the way back into the house. He found Nevina waiting for him. "Nevina?"

"John, I don't want to stay here but I need to pack up my office. Will you be around for a while?" Nevina felt Naomi's arm around around her.

"We will be. And I know that Richard and Peter are staying. Peter has called in his team. Let us help you pack your office. And your bedroom too. You need to do that. Tell us what all you want to take today with you. We can come back another day." John watched with compassion as Nevina nodded, her eyes closing to try and hold back the tears that she refused to shed.

Chapter 9

Taking the boxes from the office late that afternoon, Nickol headed for the attached garage, breaking them down and then tying them together to be put out for recycling. He sighed. Today had been far too stressful for Nevina. He could tell by how she was moving and then holding her arm. Still healing, she had just refused to quit, despite everyone's effort to ensure that she did. Heading back into the kitchen, Nichol shot a look at the clock and then reached to make sandwiches for them. A tray filled with the plate of sandwiches, a bowl of fruit, and mugs of coffee was in his hands as he headed for the office.

Nevina stared around the room. It was one of the larger rooms in the house and had been set up by Nickol for a home office. She had always liked the room, with its French door opening to a four-season sun room. That room, she decided, would soon become her favourite room. There was no question that she was walking away from Nickol, not unless he asked her to and that she didn't think would happen, not from how he was reacting to her.

"All set, sweetheart?" Nickol reached to sweep her into a hug, mindful of her shoulder.

"I am. Thank you. I'm glad it's a large room." Nevina looked around. The furniture had been shifted to allow her desk and the table that she needed for her work to be placed near a window. Nickol's desk sat nearby, close enough that they would be able to converse without raising their voices. The men had taken the time to set up her computers as she and Naomi had sorted through the other material and supplies that she had brought with her. Naomi had disappeared at one point and sorted out her clothing for her. Nevina had been grateful for her cousin's help.

"It is a large room. I always felt lost in here. Now, I don't." Nickol turned her towards the sun room. "Come on out here. We'll eat and then spend time in prayer. We need to choose to find God's peace in all this, even though we don't understand what is happening."

Monday morning, Nickol had reluctantly walked away from his home. He sensed the danger that was approaching them but had no choice. He was needed at his work. Nevina had watched him drive away before the doors were locked behind him. She felt unsafe that morning, not sure why but she too sensed the incoming danger to them both. She just didn't understand why.

Two hours later, Nevina looked up from the photos that she had been working on, a frown on her face. She turned instead to her business email, working through what she had to before her hand stopped on the mouse. Shoving herself back from the desk, Nevina tumbled to the floor and lay there, her arms covering her head before she was on her feet, running through the house, ensuring that the windows and doors were indeed locked up tight. That email had been a threat against her and against Nickol. Who threatened to kill them? Nevina searched for John's office email and sent the threatening email to him. She didn't know if he was working that day or not but he needed to have that.

John was on his feet as soon as he had read the email, searching for an officer to send Nevina's way and then searching for Jerome.

"Jerome? Got a moment?" John hesitated as he approached Jerome in a conference room.

Jerome looked around, see the worry and agitation that John normally didn't show.

"What's up?" He shoved back a chair with his foot, waiting for John to sit.

"Here. Take a look at this." John handed over the printed email. "Nevina just got this, she said. It's nasty."

Jerome searched John's face before his eyes dropped to the email. He read it and then read it again.

"She's right. It is nasty. Where do we stand with that investigation?" Jerome had not been able to keep up with that investigation for the last couple of days, off on some vacation time.

"Not where I would like it. We have no idea who either party is who has become involved. Nickol and Nevina are not able to identify them. The house where they were last kept? It has been sold to a numbered company in the last couple of months. I spoke to the old owner. He had no idea who the new owner was. He just sold it and moved out of town." John was frustrated by that.

"I see. And Emma is working this, I gather?" At John's nod, Jerome sat back in his chair, a finger tapping at the paper. "And where do we go from here with this? You've sent it on to the lab?"

"I have. They're swamped right now but will get to it as soon as they can. Hopefully, nothing happens to either Nickol or Nevina in the meanwhile." John was on his feet, walking away, needing to be on a crime scene but he fully intended on tracking Nevina down that day.

Nickol quietly closed the garage door into the house behind him that afternoon. He could hear soft sounds from further inside the house, a smile lighting his face. It had been a hard day, he decided, finding the dead fox kits. Someone had done that deliberately and now an investigation had to be gotten underway. He had turned what information he had over to his boss, who had stared at him and then shook his head. Nickol had been asked if they were the same kits that Nevina had photographed that day. He had stared at the man standing in front of him before he shook his head. They were not, he confirmed, but who had done that was what he wanted to know.

Nevina turned as she felt an arm around her and Nickol's kiss on her temple. She could grow to like this, she decided.

"Have a good day, sweetheart?" Nickol studied the lady in his arms, sensing that she was troubled. "What happened?"

"A nasty email." Nevina stopped him from moving towards the office. "I sent it on to John and he tracked me down a while ago. Let's eat and then find our prayer corner. I'll let you see it only then." She hugged him and then moved away, heading for the kitchen.

Nickol watched her walk away before he headed for a shower and his comfy clothes as he called them. Returning to stand just outside of the kitchen, Nickol studied Nevina, seeing the subtle signs that she was scared. He had no idea how to help her other than to pray for her and beg God's protection on the lady who he now admitted that he loved.

"Nevina?" Nickol reached to help set the table before he stopped his lady, simply holding her. He could feel the terror that she was trying hard to hold back. "We need to talk about what happened. I don't know that we'll be able to eat until we do."

Nevina leaned back to stare up at him before she nodded, reaching for the paper that she had set on the countertop.

"Here. Read this. Then we pray. I'm terrified, Nickol. John wasn't able to give much advice, unfortunately."

Nickol's eyes didn't move from her face as he took the paper. He pulled out a chair, sat, and then pulled her down on his lap, his arms around her as his head bowed. He prayed harder than he had ever prayed, Nickol decided. This was his lady who seemed to have been threatened.

Reaching for the paper once more, Nickol read the threat, fear rising within him. Who was behind this? He didn't have a clue, he decided, but needed to find out. This had gone too far.

"What did John actually say?" Nickol waited patiently for Nevina to respond.

"Not a lot. He did say that the lab had it and would work on tracing the email but he didn't know if that would even be possible. Somehow, I doubt that they'll be able to track it. I'm scared, Nickol. You're out there on your own." She studied him. "What happened today?"

"I found some fox kits that had been killed. No, not the ones that you photographed. Another family of kits. I didn't find the mother and that worries me." Nickol sighed. "And then there's this."

"How do we stay safe, Nickol? How do we do that? You're out on your own in the forest. I'm out and about doing what I need to. We can't just hide at home." Nevina chewed at her lower lip.

"I know, sweetheart. I know. We'll talk with Peter and Richard. Naomi will have some good advice as well." Nickol shoved away from the table, on his feet, his hand reaching for Nevina's. "Let's find our prayer corner, sweetheart. We need that more than we need to eat."

Chapter 10

A week had passed since Nevina had received that email. Peter or one of his team had been around, searching the property daily without finding anything nasty as Nevina put it. Nickol walked away reluctantly each day, fearing each day would find Nevina disappearing on him and not being found. Nevina watched him walk away from her with the same feeling.

Out and about in the town, Nevina turned that morning, hearing her name called. Emma Finlay was walking towards her, a man that Nevina didn't know beside her.

"Nevina! Just the person I was looking for." Emma hugged her, standing back and assessing her friend. "Just where are you heading?"

Nevina shrugged, not sure where she had been going.

"I'm not sure, Emma. I just needed to get away from my work for a while." Nevina gave a half smile. "But you're in my town. Why?"

Emma grinned at her again before linking an arm with her and drawing her into a nearby cafe.

"In here, Nevina. We'll share a meal and then we'll head back to your house. You're walking." Emma had no doubt that Nevina was doing just that.

"I am. I needed to. Do you understand?" Nevina frowned at Emma for a moment.

"I do, Nevina. More than you know. Listen. Micah here wants to check out your computer. He's our computer whiz. For now, let's eat and talk about anything other than what you are going through." Emma looked around for the server who was heading their way with menus.

An hour later, Micah nodded at Emma as he sat down in front of Nevina's computer. Abe's team had discussed the situation and decided that this needed to be done. He would also search the interior of the house for anything that didn't belong. They were certain that cameras and that kind of stuff, as Nathaniel so eloquently put it would be found.

Emma drew Nevina away to the sun room, looking around at how comfortable and cozy it was.

"I like this room, Nevina." Emma wandered the room, her hand touching ornaments and plants.

"I do too. Nickol had it set up when I moved in here." Nevina drew in a deep quivering breath. "We don't understand, Emma. Why us?"

"We're not getting a good sense as to why yet, Nevina. And I should be. That's very concerning. Whoever it is that is after you is hiding well." Emma sat on the love seat, facing her friend.

"That's what we're afraid of, that someone in the police are involved and monitoring what is going on." Nevina and Nickol had discussed that very issue the night before. Nickol had agreed with his bride that

—

they needed to broach that question with John or Jerome. "Nickol is going to speak with either John or Jerome. Someone is hiding information, we think, and hindering that investigation."

"That is entirely possible. I have seen it too many times to recount." Emma reached for one of Nevina's hand, simply bowing her head to pray for her friend, bringing in all the verses that she could about protection and peace. "You don't have peace in your situation and fight, Nevina. You need to choose that."

Nevina blew out a deep breath. Emma was so right, she decided. Neither one of the couple had the peace of God that they needed.

"We are praying that way, Emma. It's just so hard to trust when you're in danger." Nevina looked up as she heard footsteps. "Micah? What did you find?"

"Surprisingly, nothing. We thought that we might. You have good security on your computer. Now, your house? That's another story. Someone has managed to place some listening devices and cameras around the outside but not inside. Did anyone ever search?"

Nevina nodded, knowing that the house was searched both inside and outside on a daily basis.

"It's done every day. Either Richard or Peter or John make sure that they do that. So, if you have found something, it was placed when I was away. Peter was around this morning before I left. And there was no notice from the security feed that anyone was seen." Nevina was on her feet, heading back to her computer and pulling up the security feed for Micah. "If someone had been around, we would have received a notification."

Micah was back into the chair in front of the computer, working through the system.

"You're right. I see some blips for a few seconds which may be when they moved in and out. Nothing to show that anyone was around." Micah frowned as he spoke. "Let me talk with Joseph, our security guy, and see what we can do to enhance the system." He was on his feet and away from the two ladies, leaving Nevina staring after him.

"Did he just do that?" Nevina walked to where she could watch Micah.

Emma laughed but her eyes did not hold any humour. Micah was on to something, she knew, and between Joseph and himself, they would secure the house even more.

"He did but only because he needs to speak with Joseph. He will talk with you and Nickol before they do anything." Emma looked around as she heard another voice, finding Nickol moving in to hug his lady. "Nickol?"

"I know. I'm home. My boss sent me home for the rest of the week." Nickol grinned down at Nevina. "But Emma? You're here?"

"I am. Abe sent myself and Micah. Micah is working on your security system. He also found cameras and that kind of stuff outside the house. That was placed this morning when Nevina was out of the house." Emma didn't have to elaborate any more. Nickol was nodding.

"We thought that. Even though we search daily, they are still getting in close. And the security system is not alerting." Nickol looked around as Micah reappeared. "Micah?"

Micah simply shook his head. The security system had been compromised and compromised badly.

"Your security system is compromised, Nickol, Nevina. Joseph is heading this way. We're setting you up with a new system with a new company. We have to. Otherwise, this will continue until one of you disappear again." Micah didn't add that he had spoken with John who was not surprised.

"I see. Then I guess that's what we do." Nevina walked away, heading outside to pace the yard. She felt an arm around her and leaned against Nickol. Her feelings of love for him were just growing daily. She just didn't know how he felt and needed that but would never ask.

"Nevina? You're okay?" Nickol waited patiently for Nevina to nod. "We'll get there, sweetheart. We'll get there. For now, let's find a seat out here and spend time in prayer. Emma's working away on something and so is Micah. They'll make it as safe here for us as they can."

"I know that they will. I'm just afraid for your family. I finally heard from Mom and Dad. They're not able to head home just yet but will as soon as they can." She looked up at the tall man just holding her.

—

"They need to talk to us, Mom said, but she felt that it could wait until next week. I pray that she is correct."

"Your mom usually is with those feelings." Nickol thought back over the years. Nevina's mom had always been able to perceive things and people without saying how or why. That had been a gift from God that she had used to help others.

"I know she is. I just wish this was different." Nevina's emotions were in a turmoil. She had no idea how to solve that without hurting Nickol. "Nickol? Where do we go from here? I mean as a couple. This has been unfair to you."

"And unfair to you." Nickol bit at his lip, realizing that he did need to speak from his heart. "I would have chosen you, Nevina, in any event. You have always had my heart." He didn't look at her, not wanting to see her rejection.

"Do you mean that, Nickol?" Nevina waited somewhat impatiently for him to nod. "I'm so glad. I thought I was the only one who felt like that/."

Nickol stared down at the lady in his arms, grateful that God had placed her in his life. It now seemed as if she would be in his life for however long that they lived.

"We'll talk more, sweetheart, when we're alone. For now, let's spend some time in prayer. We're really going to need that." Nickol was as good as his word, his head bending as he prayed.

Nevina's head bowed as well as her hands tightened on her groom's. She felt some peace in the situation at last.

Chapter 11

A week later, they were no further ahead in the investigation than they had been. Every lead and tip that John and Jerome had been handed or discovered on their own had led to nowhere. They were both frustrated at that. Emma had been doing her best but even she had not found out what she should have and usually did by this time into an investigation. She had talked at length with both investigators and with her friend a police detective in her town. None of them could explain what was going on.

Abe finally turned one day, facing his Uncle Eddie Brown, a retired detective who had appeared in his work office.

"Abe? This bit with Nickol and Nevina? How far along is the investigation?" Eddie waited patiently for Abe to speak, knowing that his nephew would think it through before he did that.

"It's frustrating, Eddie. We are getting nowhere, none of us. Even John and Jerome are frustrated." His eyes narrowed as he stared at his uncle. "What are you thinking?"

"That someone is after Nickol, but didn't his friends undergo something as well?" At Abe's nod, Eddie rubbed at his cheek. "What if, as with you, someone was after each one of them but after all of them as well? Would that happen to them? I don't know them or their town."

———

"It's the rumblings that I'm hearing from Slavin's Shaye and Roane's Ragen. Nevina is chiming in as well, given how she knows the stories of the two other couples. She is convinced that the other two ladies are onto something. They just don't know what." Abe shifted how he was sitting on the corner of his desk, looking around his uncle as the door to the office opened. "Ben? You're here too?"

"I am. I came out with Eddie but wanted to speak with Micah first, given how he's been working with Joseph on that security system. I can tell you that the company is no longer in business. The owners have been charged with crimes up to and including theft." Ben shook his head at Eddie. There was more that they needed to discuss between them. "What we would like to do, Eddie and I, is to head that way on a presumed vacation. Peg and Marg go with us." Peg was Eddie's wife's, Marg Ben's. "That way, as tourists, we can slip in and around the town. We'll contact Nickol and Nevina as friends of yours. That should work."

Abe stared at his uncle and then at Ben, another retired officer. He shook his head. Ben and Eddie were on to something, he suspected.

"How many retired officers and current officers do you two know over there?" Abe waved his hands. "No, don't tell me. A lot. It could be dangerous for you all."

"We are well aware of that, Abe." Eddie perched on the corner of another desk. "We have spent the last week just in prayer for this step, all four of us. We are agreed that we need to do this. You are not aware, but Rebecca does know Nevina to some degree from their shared work of photography. I didn't know that until yesterday, She is quite concerned about her friend and is ready to pack up herself and Gideon and head that way. Gideon has already started his own investigation into it, using his own resources as well as those of Sidney's. This goes a lot deeper that what we can even imagine. Frankie has been in touch with John, just to offer what our force can." Frankie was a good friend as well as a police detective, having spent years as an undercover officer on the streets of their town.

"I see. When do you plan to leave?" Abe looked around as the other seven of his team entered and then just stood around the two older men.

"Tomorrow. I can't say how long we will be gone for. That depends on what we find. You know that only too well." Eddie looked around at the team, all the younger men good friends. Eddie and Ben were mentors to the men in more than just work. They were willing to pray for and with each of the men, spending time in the study of God's Word as they needed to.

The next morning, Nevina looked around from where she stood on the front porch, a frown momentarily on her face before she was running towards the two couples, Nickol shocked at her response before he was after her. He watched as she hugged each one.

"Nickol?" Nevina reached for his hand and drew him forward. "These two gentleman are retired officers from Riverville. You know? That town that Abe and Emma are from?" She grinned as the two couples laughed. "This is Eddie and his wife, Peg. They are aunt and uncle to Abe and his sister, Rebecca.

You've heard me speak of her over the years. In fact, you have met her. And this is Ben and his wife, Marg. They're here for a reason. Come on in. I don't feel safe out here."

Nickol's arm around his wife drew her that way, his eyes on the car that was parked down the street. It didn't belong there. Eddie and Ben shared a look before Eddie had noted the plate number and forwarded it to Frankie, who he knew would forward it to whoever it was that was the investigator here.

"So, Eddie, Ben? Did Abe send you?" Nevina grinned at the two men even as the two older ladies laughed.

"No, actually, he didn't. He would have had he thought of it first." Eddie reached for his mug of coffee, sipping at it before he put it back on the table. "Let us pray for you two first. Then we'll talk. We are here to help."

An hour later, Nickol was on his feet, heading for his office to retrieve his laptop and also pads of paper and pens. He just knew that they would need them. He stopped for a moment in the hallway, his eyes on Nevina as she laughed and teased the older couple. She was good friends with them, he could tell. That was something he wanted to rectify. He wanted to be friends with them as well, just to add that to his life with Nevina. Nickol jumped as he felt an arm across his shoulder. Nigel stood beside him as did his parents. He looked past them to see Nevina's parents, Trevor and Ruth, there as well, reaching to hug him before moving in on their daughter.

———

Nevina looked up as she heard familiar footsteps and then was on her feet to hug her parents. They were just who was needed, she decided, looking around the room.

"I think that we need to move to another room, people. The office, Nickol?" She looked around her mother to find Nickol standing near her, reaching to hug her.

"I think so, or the sun room. How be we try the sun room first? If we need to, we can move to the office." Nickol waited for the group to move off before he was reaching for trays for the coffee and tea that had been requested. He turned slightly to watch Nevina, seeing the troubled look on her face and the fear lurking in her eyes. Nickol sighed, only able to pray for his lady and sweetheart. They needed to solve this and soon. He was deeply afraid that he would lose his lady.

Late that evening, Nickol locked the house door behind Nigel, having watched as all of the people who seemed to have invaded their home had left. Nevina had handed over the keys and security passcode to Eddie and Ben, telling them to make her home their base. She was fine with that. Nickol was now on a search for his lady, not finding her where he had expected to. He snapped his fingers and headed for the sun room, finding her standing in the centre of the room, lost in thought. His arms coming around her startled her for a moment before she turned to him.

Nevina looked up at the tall man holding her, wonder once more in her heart that they were together. It had been a hope from her childhood that they would marry but that she had buried way down deep in her heart, not expecting it to come true. She was not prepared, however, for Nickol to bend and kiss her and then whisper that he loved her so much. Nevina could only repeat those words, knowing that they were both speaking from their hearts.

Nickol turned her towards a seat, sitting and then wrapping her close to himself. He had listened over the afternoon as Eddie and Ben had gone over all the material that seemed to have amassed. Eddie had laughed as he commented that Emma was starting to find details and was passing them along to both the couple and to the investigators. What else was she to do, Ben had asked, a grin on his own face.

"Okay, sweetheart?" Nickol waited patiently for Nevina to speak. When she didn't, he tilted his head and then gave a sad smile. She was asleep, not sleeping at night. He had heard her pacing, pacing himself in his bedroom. His head went down on hers as he began to pray, to beg God for protection, to be hidden in the hollow on the rock and covered there with God's hand. Even more than that, Nickol prayed for peace. He was making a deliberate decision to choose peace. He knew that Slavin had deliberately chosen life and Roane had chosen joy. This was what he felt strongly he needed to choose. Nevina had already expressed that was what she was seeking, peace from God.

An hour later, the door bell rang, disturbing Nickol. He sighed before he stood, carefully shifting Nevina until she was laying down and reached to cover her. He rubbed at the back of his head as he headed for the door, standing and staring out of the window before he unlocked the door to let Peter and John inside.

"What are you two doing here?" He squinted at his watch. "It only six in the evening. Aren't you supposed to be at home?"

"We are." Peter grinned at him. He held up a bag of food. "We wanted to share a meal with you two and then pray for you. We're here as friends only."

"Thank you. Nevina is sound asleep and I would rather not awaken her." Nickol peeked at the meals. "Good. You brought her a cold meal. I'll put it in the fridge for her." He turned to study his friends. "You're here for more than that, John."

—

John sighed. Nickol had read him too well, he decided.

"I am. I spoke with Frankie. He staid that Eddie and Ben are here." John reached for the cutlery that they needed for their chicken dinners.

"They are. Right now, they and their wives are at Nevina's home. She's opened it for them. And they spent all afternoon with us, going over everything. They left a pile of material into office for you." Nickol shook his head. "We eat first, I think, John. You're off duty. You need to set aside your cases for now"

John nodded. Nickol had read him correctly. He did need to do just that.

"You're correct, Nickol. I do need to do that. I hear rumblings from Ragen that we're meeting on Saturday to work on this." John grinned at Nickol who had stared back at him before nodding. "It's hard to do, though, when it is a friend. I tend to become too wrapped up in them."

"And you have been injured before because of friends. You need to step back a bit, John, just for a few days. You have vacation coming up, don't you?" Peter nodded at Nickol, knowing that John did indeed have vacation time coming that he was told that he had to take. He was planning on finding somewhere out in the boonies as he put it to relax.

"I do. I just don't like leaving any of the investigations that I'm working on."

"They will be here when you return, until they are solved." Peter reached for the garbage from their meal, crumpling it together and dropping it into the trash. Sitting back down, he folded his hands together on the table top, his attention on them. "Talk to us, Nickol. How do we pray for you two?"

Nichol stared down at his own hands, not sure how to respond. He knew what he wanted. He just wasn't sure what God's will was for them.

"For God's will, I think, John and Peter. For safety and protection for all of us, including you as an investigator. But what we are both praying for? For God's peace. We need that in what we are facing. Both of us feel strongly about it. And then too, we need to pray as we work on our relationship. We both love another and have acknowledged that to ourselves and to our families." He looked up at a sound from John. "John?"

"You two have always been a couple, you know, even as kids. You looked out for one another and you protected Nevina as much as she would allow you to. She did the same for you even when you didn't know that." John shook his head. "We always wondered when you two would realize that." John's voice died away as he frowned.

"John?" Peter had been watching his cousin closely. "What did you just figure out?"

"What did I figure out? What if they were made to marry not to destroy them, but to protect them. Nickol? Where the same men around you all the time?" John reached for a pad of paper sitting near him and reached for his pen, his eyes on his friend.

Nickol stared in shock at John even as he felt a hand on his shoulder and he reached a barn arm around to draw Nevina down beside him.

"John, what are you asking exactly?"

"Listen to me for a moment. What if there were two parties involved in that abduction? One meant you harm. Another party found you, made you marry to protect you, and then freed you. Is that possible?" John waved his hands. "I'm not even sure what I'm asking or saying."

Nevina's hand rested on Nickol's, stopping the restless movement of it.

"Peg asked me that just before they left. You were already outside with Eddie and Ben, Nickol. I hadn't had a chance to discuss that with you. Emma was thinking that but didn't have any information to confirm that." Nevina sighed. "It's a big stretch, but is it possible?"

"It is entirely possible, Nevina." Peter spoke up. "We have never felt comfortable that there was just one party involved in that. It hasn't made sense. This could very easily explain that. I know that Emma has been putting out feelers to see what she can find. She will not say anything until she has confirmed it one way or the other."

Chapter 13

Nevina walked around the house the next morning. It was early morning, almost too early for her to be up. She had walked away from Nickol, leaving him sleeping, a deep dreamless sleep it seemed that he needed. She was always awake early, finding that time was what she needed to spend with her Abba Father. Today was no different.

Her thoughts were troubled, Nevina decided. The discussion with John and Peter had been disturbing, to put it mildly. Neither she nor Nickol had spoken about it after the two men had left. They seemed to agree to put it aside for the night, instead spending time in prayer. Nevina turned as she heard a slight sound, a frown on her face as she searched for the source of the noise. A soft smile covered her face as she watched a tiny calico kitten scamper towards her, climbing up and cuddling down into her arms.

"Where did you come from, girl? Are you a stray? I don't know that I have seen you before. Come on. Into the house with you." Nevina walked rapidly to the house, closing and locking the door behind her, the kitten still snug in her arms. She didn't see the man running towards her, intent on taking her captive. The kitten had been a decoy for him to trap her. Only, it hadn't worked out the way that he had determined that it would. He gave a quick glance around and was gone before he could appear on the security feed.

Nickol turned from the kitchen counter, his eyes on the kitten.

"Where did you find it?" A finger came out to stroke the kitten's head, the kitten's paw coming up to stop him.

"Outside. I don't know where she came from." Nevina drew in a deep breath. "Was she a trap?"

Nickol shrugged. It was possible, he decided, but seeing the look on Nevina's face? That kitten would be going nowhere.

"We'll find her what she needs this morning. I'm glad it's the weekend. We need some time just for us." He reached to kiss his bride, laughing as the kitten shoved up between them. "You do have to share, you know, kitten."

Nevina's face was lit with laughter as well.

"She will. It's so new for her. We'll need to take her to the vet's as well. Josh should be open this morning. He won't mind." A good friend of theirs was a veterinarian and had often asked them why they had no animals. Neither one had wanted one, thinking their careers would be too hard on an animal. Watching the kitten exploring the room made them realize how wrong that they had been.

Walking through the downtown area a couple of hours later, Nickol kept Nevina's hand tight in his. He could feel the danger creeping up on them and he hated that. This should be a happy time for time, and for Nevina especially. He wanted to change how they had married but that wasn't possible. He stopped for a moment before pulling Nevina into the local jewelry store. She frowned at him as he shook his head.

"Paul? I need to see engagement rings. Nevina has a wedding band but not an engagement ring." Nickol paused, staring down at the plain gold rings that they both wore. "On second thought, I want to see wedding bands as well. We didn't choose these. This is not what I would have chosen for my bride, had I had time to make a proper decision." He shook his head at the question Nevina's face, knowing that he would explain when they were on their own.

Nevina stared at the beautiful ruby ring that Nickol had chosen, knowing exactly why he had. He had often mentioned that he would consider the lady who he married as having a price far above rubies. It seemed as that was how he felt about her. Thinking back over their friendship, Nevina realized that was how he had always treated her. She has just not noticed or if she had, she had tucked those feelings down into her heart and didn't bring them out to look after, afraid that if she did, he would walk away from her.

Nickol reached for Nevina's hand, walking rapidly back to his truck and tucking her inside. He could feel the danger that was approaching them. He turned as he heard someone calling his name, frowning as Ben approached him.

"Ben? You're looking for us?"

"I am, Nickol. We need to talk. Head for your home. We'll follow you." Ben pointed to his car. "Someone and that someone was God had us parking right beside you. Head off." He turned back to slip into the front seeatof the car, Eddie pulling out after Nickol.

"They weren't watching around them." Eddie's quiet comment had Ben nodding. Their two ladies had met with the mothers to spend time praying with those two ladies.

"No, they weren't. They're not used to that. Put Nickol out in the woods and he knows what to watch for. Nevina knows what to watch for with her photos." Ben sighed. "It's like all the others. They're in love and not really concentrating at the moment on the danger that they're in."

"I think that they are. They're just trying to live a normal life and that's not possible right at the moment."

The two older men watched as Nickol worked away on a meal for them. Nevina's attention was on the kitten as she set up the food and water bowl and then the littler box before dumping out the toys that she had found for her. Her face was lit with laughter as she watched the antics of the kitten. She desperately needed that, Ben decided.

"Okay, you two. Let's eat. Then we need to talk." Eddie's voice was quiet as he helped to set the food on the table.

Nevina nodded, her eyes meeting Nickol's for a moment. Slavin and Roane and their ladies had warned them about this.

"We do, don't we? What did we do that we shouldn't have?" Nevina's voice with its plaintive tone had the older men smiling.

"Nothing that you shouldn't have. You're newlyweds, no matter how you married. You will be out and about both together and on your own. It's expected. For now, let us eat, pray with you, and then given what we can from our perspective. Perhaps, we can give you some times that will help you two say alive and solve this." Eddie was as good as his word, bowing his head to pray for the younger couple once their meal had been shared.

—

Chapter 14

Jerome stood and watched as Eddie and Ben walked away. He had met with them earlier that day, surprised at the information that they had been able to find. They were not from his town but had still managed to find people willing to speak with them. Jerome had stared down at the thick file folder that he was handed, knowing that he now had an additional task of going through it. It couldn't wait until John was back in a week. It had to be dealt with and that meant going to Nickol and Nevina as well.

Nickol stood at his side, his arm around Nevina. They had not been surprised to see Jerome appear. They had just wanted an evening to themselves that didn't seem as if it was happening.

"Jerome? What do you have for us?" Nevina spoke at last, before she turned and headed back into the house, finding the little calico waiting somewhat impatiently for her to reappear. She gathered the kitten close before finding a seat in the living room.

Nickol's arm came around her as he sat beside her, his eyes on Jerome. That man was not here for his own health, he knew.

"Eddie and Ben? They have dug up a wealth of material for us. I don't know how they did it but they did. We are working through it. For now, let's set it aside. I just wanted to touch base with you and see how you were doing and to see if you have remembered anything else that we need to know about."

Nevina snorted, startling the kitten for a moment who raised her head and the placed on tiny white paw on Nevina's mouth.

"How are we doing? We're scared, angry, worried, and every other emotion that you can name inbetween all those. Does that answer your question?" Nevina glared at Jerome as he grinned at her.

"I get that, Nevina. That's normal to feel all that. For now, though, let me bring you up to date on what we can. Unfortunately, it's not a lot." Jerome was as good as his word, letting them know where the investigation stood. They were definitely not where they needed to be in that, but it was what it was. Jerome stayed for a while longer before he left, Nickol following him to the door and locking it after him.

Nickol stood for a moment, his head dropping from worry and fatigue before he raised it and headed to find his lady. It was getting late and they both had to be up early the next morning. He stood for a moment, leaning against the bedroom door frame before he reached to hug his lady, just holding her as sobs shook her body for a moment. Fear was beginning to wreak havoc with their emotions and neither one had any idea on how to stop that, other than to trust their Heavenly Father. And there were times that it was very hard to do just that.

The next afternoon, Nickol trudged back towards his truck, exhaustion evident in how he was moving. It had been a difficult day, finding the beaver family dead and that not from natural predators. They had been ruthlessly slaughtered and for what? There didn't seem to be a reason for it. Nickol paused beside his truck, his face raising to the sun, feeling its warmth on his chilled skin. There were days like this that he questioned if he was in the right occupation. That had been coming to his mind more and more lately. He and Nevina had begun to pray over it. Nickol's smiled. Having Nevina in his life as she was? All he could do was thank God for the blessings that she was bringing him. They were talking about where they wanted to go and where they could serve God best. For now, they were content with where they were.

A sound to his side brought Nickol's attention back to the present. He slipped behind the wheel of his truck, the doors locked after himself before he was driving away. He didn't see the men who had appeared just a few seconds too late to kidnap him. That had been their plan. The curses and loud words filled the air around them, disturbing the sounds and peace of nature before they stomped off, intent on following Nickol. Except that they didn't get far. Two police patrol vehicles moved in on them and the men were arrested, their criminal life catching up with them.

Nevina turned as she heard the door close behind Nickol before her attention was back on the photos that she was just finishing off. She knew that she would have some time before Nickol came to find her. He always cleaned up before that.

Nickol stood for a moment, mugs of coffee held in his hands as he watched his bride, a smile lighting his face. He walked forward, the mugs on the desk

---

before he had lifted her into his arms and sat back down in her chair, a small squeal coming from her and the kitten jumping down and running away. They both laughted at her antics.

"Have a good day, sweetheart?" Nickol kissed his lady, his arms tight around her. He was afraid that night and didn't know why. Something was about to happen, he decided, and he didn't want it to.

"I did. I was able to sort through and finish off some photos that needed to be done." Nevina leaned back against Nickol, an arm around his shoulders. "You didn't."

"No, I didn't. I found a family of beavers had been killed by someone and that means an investigation that I am not sure will solve it." Nickol was troubled by that. "Someone was following me all day, I think."

"And they will. You need to be so careful or you will disappear." Nevina's fear was just that, that Nickol would disappear on her and never return. "Our moms were around earlier. They want to have a family dinner in the next week or so."

"We can do that, I guess." Nickol groaned as Nevina laughed. "We can. Did they give a day yet?"

"They're thinking Sunday after church." Nevina grew quiet. This was not what she was used to. She was around her family as she needed to be but a lot of her time was spent on her own.

"You're not used to this." Nickol hugged her tighter. "We'll get there, sweetheart. If you can't do it, we'll just tell them that. You are my main priority, not a meal with family."

"I know, Nickol. I know. But we can''t isolate ourselves from them. It's what whoever it is after us would want. If we're isolated, then they have a better chance of catching us and disappearing with us." Nevina's head rested against Nickol's. She found comfort and peace from the contact with her fellow as she called him.

"It is likely that would happen. We can't be totally safe, no matter how much we work on that." Nickol was frustrated. John was back from vacation and working on all of his cases. They just didn't have the one piece of information that they needed to solve this case.

"John was around too. He's overwhelmed, you know. He says that they have too many cases and can't solve some of them. Is this on purpose?" Nevina was thinking aloud.

Nickol nodded. That was exactly what he thought, that there were too many cases and that was being done on purpose to confound each one.

"I think that you are correct, sweetheart. It happened with both Slavin and Roane." Nickol bit at his lip. "We need to meet with those two couples. Hearing their story again is just what we both need."

Chapter 15

A few days later, Nickol walked towards where he had found the dead beaver family, a co-worker, Geoff, by his side. He seemed to be hyper-vigilant, expecting something to happen that day and afraid of just that would be. A hand out stopped Geoff from moving past the edge of the trees. Nickol searched the area, his head moving as he did so, hearing the sound of faint conversation and noise reaching to him.

Geoff pointed to the right and Nickol nodded. They would be able to make their way around towards the beaver dam while still under cover. And Nickol had to admit to himself that he was deeply afraid. At the moment, all he could do was pray for protection for the two of them.

Nickol paused near to where the dam was, his eyes on the three men working away. He felt Geoff's hand on his shoulder for a moment before it tightened and then dropped.

"They're destroying the dam." Geoff's voice was barely audible.

"I know. I can't think why. That would be why the beavers were killed." Nickol's voice was equally low. "I don't get it." His phone was out to film the activity as was Geoff's. Neither man had discussed that between themselves. They just knew it was needed just so no one could say that Nickol had staged it.

—

Geoff looked around before he pointed to the right.

"I'll head over that way a bit and see if I can get a better look at their faces." He frowned. "They do look familiar."

Nickol nodded before his eyes slid closed. His co-worker looked at him, at the men and then back at him.

"Nickol?"

"We know them, Geoff. We had to have them arrested two years ago because of poaching. Now what are they up to?" Nickol shook his head before he moved away, his thoughts briefly turning to Nevina and praying that she was safe. He didn't feel good about that day, sensing that something was about to happen. Nickol prayed for his bride and then for their family and friends. Somehow, he knew that something was about to go bad and go bad quickly.

Geoff paused for a moment, hearing a faint sound before he shrugged. It had sounded like Nickol's voice but that wouldn't be right, now would it. His attention returned to the men working away, frowning as he realized that there were only two there at present. Where had the third one gone?

His heart froze for a moment as he recognized Nickol being shoved forward, his hands cuffed in front of him. Nickol was staggering, showing that his capture had not been easy. How had that happened in such a short period of time? Geoff crouched down, his eyes searching for a way to get closer to the activity and not seeing any way that was possible. All he could do was pray for his friend and then continue to film what he could.

An hour later, Geoff had managed to work his way carefully around to where Nickol had last been. He stopped, his hand reaching for the backpack on the ground and Nickol's cap. He tucked the cap inside the pack and then reached for Nickol's phone and tucked that into a pocket on his jacket. Geoff knew that there was no way to follow the men and Nickol, not at this point and not on his own. All he could do was pray for his friend and then turn and almost run for where he had left his truck.

Speeding away, Geoff reached for his phone. No, he wasn't to be using it while driving but this was an emergency. He quickly gave what information that he could, not realizing the consternation and worry that would ensue.

John was on his feet in the break room, heading towards Jerome. Jerome's pace was fast and angry.

"Jerome?" John's head shook in the negative. "Which one?"

"Nickol. He was out with Geoff where he found the beavers the other day. They had separated to try and determine what some men were up to. Nickol has been taken captive, Geoff has advised. We're heading out that way. I need you to head for Nevina. She's not going to take this well." Jerome watched with compassion as John's eyes slid closed. "I called Peter. He can't make it to be with her or their families. Don and Richard and their teams are in town, without knowing just why they were needed."

—

"God did that, Jerome. He had to have." John ran for his car, heading for Nevina, praying for his friend and then his friend's bride. This was not what was to have happened.

Niall turned from closing the door after John, a frown on his face. As far as he knew, John was not to have been there that day. Niall's eyes closed, shutting out the soft peach of the entry way walls before he opened them again.

"Nickol?" He didn't ask much more.

John nodded, looking around for Nevina.

"Nevina?"

"She's off with her mom and Nickol's mom. She needed to get out of the house." Niall sighed. "What happened?"

"Nickol was out with Geoff today, I gather, near where he found the dead beavers. I don't know all of the details but they separated to watch some men. Nickol was taken captive. Geoff headed back in for help." John was frustrated. He wanted to be out there on the search but couldn't. In fact, he had to head back to the department shortly for interviews that had been arranged on other cases. "I can't stay long, Niall, but there will be someone around here for the next while."

Niall locked the door after John an hour later. They had discussed the situation but neither man had a solution or an answer. His hand resting against the door, Niall's head bowed as he prayed for his son and then Nevina. The three ladies were due home soon and he didn't look forward to telling Nevina that Nickol was missing. He had glimpsed Richard and Don around the property but not all of their team members. His best guess was that some had been dispatched to find the ladies and watch out over them.

Chapter 16

Staring in horror at Niall, Nevina's head began to shake. She could feel her mother's arm around her, supporting her from collapsing to the floor. Ami stood on her other side, an arm around her as well.

"That can't be, Niall. That can't be. He was only to be out there for a short while with Geoff. How?" Nevina's voice trembled with the terror that she was feeling and was laced with the tears that she didn't know were flowing down her face.

"Geoff saw it, Nevina. He wasn't able to prevent it." Niall watched with compassion as the young lady in front of him crumpled even more. "Jerome was heading that way. John will be back around when he can. For now, Richard and Don and their teams are here."

Ami nodded at Ruth before she walked towards Niall, wrapped into his hug. She struggled with her own emotions. She could hear Nevina's father closing the door behind him as he entered, his eyes on his wife and then his daughter.

"Nevina? Love? What's happened?" Trevor wrapped his ladies into a hug.

"Nickol has gone missing, Dad. John was around when we were out." Sobs broke out, huge, heavy, heartbroken sobs that chilled the two sets of parents at their intensity.

"Come on, love. Let's find some seats and spend time in prayer. God is with us and He is most certainly with Nickol. He will protect your sweetheart." Trevor nudged his daughter to a seat on the living room couch, sitting on one side of her as Ruth sat on the other. He watched as Niall and Ami found seats, not surprised to see Nigel appear.

An hour later, Trevor sat, his head handing low for a moment. He could feel the presence of God in the room and knew that the others would as well. It was time to make some plans. Only, he had no idea what sort of plans that they could make.

Richard and Don hesitated in the doorway to the living room, trays in their hands. They had gone ahead and prepared a light lunch for the group, knowing that none of them would feel like eating. They shared a glance between them. This was where their expertise would come in as plans were made.

Niall looked around and nodded at the two men. Good, he thought. Food and then planning. John and Peter needed to be there but couldn't be. That was okay, he decided.

"Richard? Don? You are here for more than just a meal with us." Nigel rose to help pass out the food.

"We are, Nigel. Let's eat first and then we will plan." Richard's attention was on Nevina, seeing her picking at her sandwich without really eating. He rose at last as did Don to clear away the food remnants, returning with the tray of coffee pot and tea pot and what was needed for their drinks. "Let me pray with you, Nevina." Richard didn't wait for her to nod. He simply bowed his head and prayed, ending with his usual "I love You". It was how he always did that, stating that God loved them and He needed to hear that He was loved even though He did know that.

"Now what? Richard? Don?" Niall spoke for the group, knowing the men the best of the two fathers.

"Now what? We make plans and more than one set of plans. We don't know yet why Nickol was taken. That's what Jerome and John are working on. Emma is weighing in as well but she has been called out with Abe and his team." Richard reached for the folders that he had set to one side. "Here. This is what we have come up with, between Peter, Abe, Don, and myself. As always, it's just a working form. Things can and will change what we do. The main thing is to keep Nevina safe. We don't understand yet why Nickol was taken, whether it's related to his job or to something else or how Nevina plays into it."

Don spoke up, his eyes on Nevina.

"Nevina? Did you ever determine why you two were forced to marry? We've discussed this before without any real consensus."

"No, I don't know that we did. Our feeling at one point was that someone had done it to protect us, but we have no proof." She swiped at her face, taking with thanks the warm cloth that Ami had retrieved for her.

"That's what we have been discussing with our teams. Now, Richard here was forced to marry Raleigh. Not many are aware of that." Don waited for the murmurs to die down again. "If you need to talk

---

with someone, she's willing to do that. Or we have other friends who will speak with you." Don sipped at his mug of coffee before he set it to one side again. His eyes studied the warmer peach tones of the living room walls, the dark hardwood floors, the cream trim and the patterned drapes. He liked the sense of peace that was present in the room.

"So, how do we do this, Don?" Trevor spoke up, his eyes on his daughter. "How do we keep Nevina safe and yet allow her freedom? And how do we find out where Nickol is?"

"Those are good questions, Trevor." Richard handed out the papers that he had been rolling in his hands. "These suggestions are a start. And Nevina, we are well aware that you need to be out and about. Just not on your own for now. We have worked out a schedule among our four teams to have two members with you at all times when you are out." Richard's hand went up. "I know. You can't afford us." He grinned as she scowled at him. "There is never a charge for friends, Nevina. And our ladies have all expressed a desire to meet with you and Ami and Ruth if that is what you want."

Nevina nodded. She had been feeling very isolated and scared, no terrified, she decided.

"I would like that. It's up to Mom and Ami if they do. But for now? How do we find Nickol?" Her face and voice were sober, just a hint of the tears she was trying so hard to control coming through.

"That's what we need to discuss." Don did just that, laying out scenarios and solutions. "Of course, not knowing where he is or why or who has him does complicate what we do.”

The two team leaders rose at last and walked away, stopping to stare back at the house.

“She’s going to run out on her own. You do know that?” Don grinned as Richard shook his head. “All our ladies did that.”

“I know. I just wish that she wouldn’t. All we can do is try our best with God’s help to protect her and find Nickol.”

Chapter 17

Nickol's head hung low. It had been a week since he had been tackled to the ground, a lucky blow knocking him senseless for a few moments, just long enough for him to be handcuffed and then hauled viciously to his feet. He had stumbled as he had been forced forward, not knowing who had taken him captive or why.

Shoved to the ground, Nickol had waited for someone to approach him and tell him why he was handcuffed. His hands were raised as he swiped at the blood on his cheek, his eyes clearing somewhat as he studied the men in front of him. Nickol frowned. One of the men didn't seem to fit but that couldn't be right. He couldn't hear the conversation that was ongoing even as they finished destroying the dam and letting the water run free. That he couldn't understand. The water would go nowhere other than down into the local creek.

The men turned at last, watching him before another argument broke out. That he had not been wanted as a captive was obvious but they couldn't let him go. He had seen their faces and heard their voices and as such, he could certainly be a witness against them.

Nichol had once more been hauled to his feet and then shoved viciously forward again along an animal trail, one man ahead of him, the other two behind him.

They carried their tools of destruction over their shoulders. He desperately looked for a way to escape but couldn't find one. He was suddenly afraid, afraid for Nevina and afraid that he would not be returning to her.

Sitting in the back seat of a truck, Nickol tried hard to memorize what way they were heading, that was until a blindfold dropped over his eyes. He sighed to himself. It would be impossible now to figure out where he was. He felt the truck stop and then a hand on his arm yanking him out of the truck and then forward. Nickol stumbled up some steps and then tripped over the entry to the house, barely staying on his feet. The hand shoved him forward, something that he was getting very tired of and into a room, the door slamming shut behind him. Nickol heard the lock snick closed and then waited. He had no idea where he was or why. Finally, his cuffed hands reached for the blindfold and dropped it to the floor.

Gazing around, Nickol reached for the door. It was locked, just as he suspected. The windows were also fastened shut in a way that he could not access them to open them. He turned, his cuffed hands clasped together. This was not a scenario that he was happy with but he didn't have any choice in the matter. All he could do at present was pray for God's protection and safety. His thoughts turned to Nevina and he begged God to protect her as well.

Nickol waited for someone to reappear but no one did. Dusk came and then night fell, without anyone bringing him any food. He had been able to scoop water into his hands from the bathroom sink and drink, at least getting some fluid into himself. He turned and paced the room, finally sinking down on the bed and stretching out. His eyes closed and Nickol slept, not hearing the door open and someone appear. The man who didn't seem to fit walked towards Nickol, assessing him and then staring behind him at the door. He needed to get Nickol out of there but there was just no chance. The tray of food had been set on the small table near the bed before the man walked away. He was under too much of a watch himself to try anything yet.

Nickol roused the next morning, scrubbing at his face, forgetting for a moment that he was a captive. He stared at his hands, still handcuffed together, before he was on his feet, searching once more for a way out of the room. There just was no way. His attention focused on the tray of food sitting on the table and he froze. Someone had been in the room when he had been asleep. That scared Nickol. He had no idea if that man meant to harm him or not.

Days passed like this until the week had ended. Nickol had not been released from his handcuffs, as much as he had asked for that when the young man had appeared. That man had simply stared at Nickol and shaken his head. Their employer was adamant on that. Nickol was not to be freed at any time. The man, not wanting to admit even to himself, was scared of Nickol and what he could do. He had watched Nickol for years from afar, waiting for the perfect opportunity to take him captive and force him to work for their organization. He just didn't think that it would take that long. That man had stood in the shadows of the hallway at times, watching as the room was entered and the trays of food exchanged. He heard the questions that Nickol fired at the man, questions that he hadn't expected Nickol to ask. His whole expectation was that Nickol would crack in a day and willingly work for him. That was how it aways went.

Nickol paced the bedroom that day at the week's mark. He was frustrated, tired, sore of being shackled, and not ready to give in. He was a realist, knowing that whoever had captured him was waiting for just that. Instead, Nickol had spent his days in prayer and waiting before his Abba Father, quoting to himself all the Bible verses that he had memorized over the years. His thoughts would go to Nevina and he would beg God to protect his beloved lady and keep her safe.

That day, Nickol had stood just to the side of the door as it opened and the young man appeared, a tray in his hand. A sudden shove from Nickol had the man flying forward to land on the floor, the tray and its contents spewing across the floor as well. Nickol ran for the door, his feet pounding across the wooden floors as he reached for the handle on the front door and yanked it open, flying through the doorway and towards safety. His feet sank into the soft lawn, impeding him to some degree. Yells of rage rang out behind him and he sensed the men chasing him. He prayed that he could escape. Only, that was a distant wish that didn't happen.

The older man flung himself through the air, his arms around Nickol's waist as he tackled him to the ground. A leaden fist landed on Nickol's jaw, sending him spiralling down into darkness. The man was on his feet, pacing around Nickol, anger raging from him.

—

"How did he get out?" That man spun to confront the younger man.

The younger man raised his hands and shook his head.

"He was waiting for me when I opened the door. He shoved me forward before I could even see where he was. He would have done the same to you." He reached for one of Nickol's arm as the other man reached for the other.

Nickol was dragged back towards the house, his head dangling down and bobbing the the movement of his body. His feet dug into the soft lawn before catching on the stones of the walk and then the edges of the stairs. Nickol did not rouse at all as he was dragged back into the house . His feet continued to drag along the wooden floor before his body was dropped to the bedroom floor, his cuffed hands beneath him. The older man paced around the room, his anger directed towards Nickol. He approached the unconscious man before his booted foot was back and then driven into Nickol's side. A groan came from Nickol before he was once more still. The two men backed out of the room, the door locked behind them.

This was not how the day was to have gone. Nickol was to have been brought to the office where he would meet with their employer and be given the opportunity of working for him or death. That confrontation would now have to wait. And both men knew that the man's anger would be great and directed at them.

Chapter 18

That night or was it the next morning, Nickol roused. He was not sure what time of day it was, only that it was dark. He rolled to his side, a hand reaching for his side before the other hand reached to rub at his eyes. He stared at his hands, not comprehending that he was handcuffed, only that his hands didn't work the way that he thought they should. Nickol shoved himself to his feet, staggering for a moment as he regained his balance and then headed for the ensuite, the sink taps turned on to run as warm of water as he felt that he could handle.

Nickol stared at himself in the mirror, seeing the large ugly-looking bruise on his jaw and the rumpled look about himself. He sighed. He had no idea what had happened to him or why. Staring down at his hands, Nickol was even more puzzled as to why he was handcuffed. He turned, stumbling as he made his way to the bed and sank down on it. He was out of it again, as he would later put it, before he had even settled down.

The young man unlocked the door, looking behind him the next day. He had been in and out of Nickol's room the day before on orders of his boss, who wanted Nickol on his feet and to face him. That wasn't happening. That had only increased the man's rage and caused all his employees to disappear as they could to avoid his vile temper.

—

The man looked behind him at the open door and then back at Nickol. For the moment, he was alone in the house with Nickol. Their employer had left for a few days, taking the other man with him. Any other employees avoided the house when he was away, not wanting to be around the vileness that filled the building. He reached to shake Nickol's shoulder, not surprised when Nickol barely roused.

He coaxed Nickol to his feet and then with an arm around him, guided him to the door, hesitating to lock it behind him and then walked out of the house and towards the back of the yard, knowing that he had tampered with the security system just long enough for him to get Nickol away. Shoving Nickol down into his car, the man, Jonathan by name, looked around before he was behind the wheel and speeding away, away from the house and away from the town that Nickol called home. He needed to get Nickol back on his feet and to the authorities but he was afraid to do that in this town. Someone was spying for the employer and that scared Jonathan.

Jonathan drove around for a while before heading for the town of Riverville. It was his home town, although not many in his life now knew that. He had kept that hidden, undercover as he was with the man that he was now fleeing from with Nickol. It would not go well with him if he was caught, that much he was certain of. His eyes kept flicking to watch Nickol, concerned that Nickol had not really roused and even now just slumped in the car seat. Pulling the vehicle over to the side of the road, Jonathan's fingers tapped at the wheel. It was now dusk, which he had been waiting for. His phone was out as he sent a text message to a friend, receiving the affirmative response that he had expected.

Driving up to a house, Jonathan's hand reached for the light switch for the vehicle's high beams and flicked them on and off briefly. The garage door in front of him opened slowly to allow him passage into the garage and then just as slowly closed behind him. Jonathan was out of the vehicle, around the car to open Nickol's door and pulling him out and to his feet, an arm around him once more as he navigated through the garage and then into the house and through the mud room and to the kitchen.

John Thompson watched Jonathan briefly before he was beside the two men, his own hands helping to stabilize Nickol on his feet before he was nodding his head towards one of the spare rooms.

"In there, Jonathan. I won't ask what's going on. You'll need to talk to either Frankie or Caleb, I suspect."

"That I will, John. Thanks for this. Nickol here has been missing from his home for almost two weeks. His bride must be frantic about his whereabouts. Two days ago, he tried to escape from the house he was being held in. The other man slugged him hard. He hasn't really been awake since then. Just so you know? He was kept handcuffed all the time up until today." Jonathan didn't continue. He couldn't, not until he had talked to someone.

"I see. Then, let's see what we can do about making him comfortable. Mary has some broth in the freezer. Go ahead and pull it out. You know our kitchen well." John turned to watch Jonathan walk away, worried about his only's sister's only child. Jennifer had asked that John watch out for him when he began to live on his own before she had passed away far too soon from cancer. John had taken Jonathan under his wing, worrying that he had chosen the work that he had, as an undercover officer for a task force no one wanted to talk about, but proud of the man that his nephew had become.

Jonathan nodded, before helping his uncle settle Nickol onto a bed, turning at last to walk away. He shut the bedroom door behind him, his head resting back against it as his eyes closed. He prayed for the man who he had rescued and for his uncle who was treating him. He also prayed for Nickol's bride. He didn't know her name, not yet, but he knew that Nickol was married. The ring on his finger showed that.

John had turned to watch the door close before his attention went back to Nickol. He reached for his medical kit, a kit that he kept handy at home. He was an Emergency Room physician but didn't hesitate to step in to help if he was asked to. This time? It was the first time that his nephew had asked that of him despite John's frequent reassurances that he would help Jonathan in any way that he could.

Nickol groaned slightly as John felt for broken bones before he laid still, causing some concern for John. He reached for the IV needle that he had prepared for Nickol, inserting it into the hand nearest him and starting the rehydration process that was needed. John also cleansed the scrapes on the wrists, wrapping bandages around them as needed.

John stood back at last, concerned about Nickol but knowing that he had done the best that he could. He would work with his wife, Mary, a retired nurse who still helped out as needed. She was away for the day, not due home until the next day. That was okay, John decided. He would work with what he could.

Shutting the door behind him, John hesitated as he heard more than his nephew's voice, his head tilting to listen before he nodded. Frankie Brennen was there and that was just who was needed. Frankie was the head detective on the Riverville police force and would take Jonathan's statement that night. He would not be taking Nickol's, not that night. John was not sure when that would even happen.

Chapter 19

The two weeks that had passed had drawn from Nevina all the hope and confidence that she had had that Nickol would return to her quickly. It had just not happened. After the first week, she had sent the security teams home, just telling to go about their lives. They could not stay with her forever. They had nodded and left but not totally. She was not aware that some of them were still there, taking turns to watch out for her and to watch out for anyone who meant her harm. It was what the four teams had agreed to. John and Edward were part of that detail when they could be as well as many off-duty officers. Nickol was well liked in his town, his family working with the law enforcement teams as they needed to. Besides, as a wildlife officer, Nickol was considered part of the law enforcement community.

Nevina had struggled to work, not sleeping at night. She was barely eating and taking to hiding at home, sending her parents and Nickol's parents away, fearful that they would be harmed. Nigel had just refused to leave unless she could lock him out of the house. Slavin and Shaye and Roane and Ragen had refused to leave as well, staying as long as she would allow, working through the mass of material that they were accumulating. Emma and Abe had been around at the one-week mark, just to pray with her and share with her what they were discovering.

Staring at the wall that evening of the two-week mark, Nevina had sighed. She had prayed until she felt that she could pray no more. She had begged and wept for Nickol to return to her and that hadn't happened. Nevina had acknowledged that God was in control, that He had walked the path that they were walking already, and that He only wanted His best for them. It was hard to acknowledge, she decided, that they were not in control. All she could do that night was sigh heavily as she prepared for bed and then crept under the covers, her arms wrapping around Nickol's pillow even as sobs shook her body. She slept, a deep sleep that was needed but that she had been trying to avoid.

A dark figure crept silently through the house just after midnight, his feet silent on the hardwood floors. He searched the house for someone, not finding that person. Fear grew in his heart that Nevina had disappeared as well.

Reaching the bedroom, he paused, sensing someone in the room. Making his way to the bed, he stood, staring down at the form cuddled up under the blankets. He drew a deep breath before his hand rested on her hair and then a kiss was dropped on her cheek. Nevina roused somewhat, sensing someone near her before she slept again.

Nickol reached quickly for clean night clothes, the ensuite door closing behind him as he changed. He studied his face in the mirror, seeing the changes that had happened over the past two weeks, the dark shadows under his eyes, the whiteness of his face, the fatigue that was evident. He was not the man that he had been before his captivity. That man would never return. His head turned as he stared at the door, a prayer raising for his beloved Nevina and then for them as a couple before the light was clicked off and the door opened. Slipping under the covers, Nickol simply reached for Nevina, wrapping her in his arms before his head rested against her even as tears flowed down his cheeks. He too slept, a deep sleep that he also needed.

Nevina roused that morning, staring at the clock. It was after nine, thankfully on a Saturday. She never slept that late but the night before she had had a deep sleep. She frowned for a moment, thinking that she was not alone. She moved, finding herself trapped and unable to move any further. Fear rushed through her as she shifted as best that she could, her head turning. Nevina's movements stopped as she stared at Nickol, not sure when or even how he had appeared but he was there. She struggled to free an arm, her hand resting against his cheek, the beard that he had not shaved off as yet rough under her hand. All she could do was praise and thank God that Nickol was home.

Nickol stirred as he felt a hand on his cheek, his arms tightening around Nevina for a moment before his eyes opened, staring at the love of his life.

"Nevina? You're okay?" His voice was still rough from not being used.

"I am. Nickol? You're home! How? And when?" Nevina reached to brush the tears from his face, not realizing that tears covered her as well.

"Early this morning. We'll talk, my love, we'll talk. I need to find John at some point, I think, even though Frankie did take my statement." He studied her face, seeing the changes in it that mimicked his own. "You're okay?"

"I am. Better than okay now that you're home. The guys and gals all took care of me. I sent them home last week. Only they never left."

Nickol gave a low laugh before he kissed her.

"I am so glad to be home. We'll talk, sweetheart." He shifted in bed before he punched himself upright, shoving the pillows behind him. He studied Nevina once more. "What day is it?"

"It's Saturday." Nevina sighed as she sat up as well, cross legged on the bed. "Your family, my family, our friends, will all be around. I have not had much time to myself."

"No, you wouldn't. Abe and Nathaniel brought me home last night. I know the others were there as well. I would not be surprised if they were will here or someone else is." Nickol's eyes closed for a moment as a rush of fatigue swept through him. He felt Nevina's hand on his arm and reached for it. "I'm okay, sweetheart. It was rough."

"I can only imagine." She reached for her phone, sighing as she did so. "Nigel is on his way. That man!"

Nickol gave a low laugh even as he reached to kiss her again.

"He takes care of people, Nevina. He always has. Now, we need to get up, don't we?" He gave a grin as she shook a finger at him.

———

"We do. We'll talk at some point. Geoff was so afraid for you. You need to let him and your boss know that you're home." Nevina was away, reaching for clean clothes, and then shutting the ensuite door. She looked around, a smile on her face as she reached for the clothes that Nickol had just dropped on the floor the night before. That was not him, she knew, but she could understand to a certain extent that it was how he had reacted.

Chapter 20

Nigel shut the front door quietly behind him, a bag of food from a local coffee shop in his hand. He had no idea how many people would invade the house that day so he had come prepared, he thought. His head tilted as he heard Nevina singing softly to herself. Nigel frowned. She had not been doing that for the last couple of weeks. Something had changed. He dropped the food on the kitchen table and then stopped. Someone was behind him.

Turning to face the kitchen doorway, Nigel froze. He blinked and then rubbed at his eyes. Nickol was not standing there, he decided. It was just a mirage, a wishful dream that he was. Hearing a soft laugh, his eyes popped open once more.

"It's me, Nigel. I'm home." Nickol was across the room, his arms hugging his brother tightly even as Nigel hugged him back. "We'll talk."

"When did you get home?" Nigel stepped back even as Nevina moved in on Nickol, to be wrapped in Nickol's arms.

"Early this morning. Abe brought me home. I'll tell you what all happened. But for now? You brought food?" Nickol moved past his brother, reaching for the bags of food. "I know who it was, Nigel. Someone we both know and don't like very well. We need to work to prove it. Emma is doing that, she said, but is running into roadblocks." He set out the muffins and other food, turning as Nevina reached for his hand to tug him away for a moment.

"Nickol? You do need to eat but we need to pray first. Nigel?"

Her question had Nigel nodded, before he wrapped his brother and Nevina into a hug, his voice raised in prayer. He heard the sound of the door and then soft footsteps before those footsteps paused and then other voices picked up the prayers.

Niall stared at his sons, blinking as he realized that Nickol was there. Nickol simply moved into his father's hug and then to his mother. Trevor and Ruth were there as well to hug their son-in-law before Ruth moved to wrap an arm around her daughter. Peter and John nodded at one another. Frankie and Abe had been in touch with both of them, warning them that Nickol was home and that they needed to talk with him.

Laughter and happiness filled the house for the next while, even though there was an underlying sense of fear and concern that just couldn't be totally ignored. John watched his friend, seeing the changes in him and knowing that these changes were similar to Slavin and Roane. Those two couples had shown up as well as had Edward. Jerome had been in and out, needing to be on a crime scene but he had studied Nickol intently, nodding at John who nodded back. They would both speak with that man, just to get a sense of what he knew and what had happened. They always did that with victims.

Nickol turned at last, heading for his office, an arm around Nevina. Neither one was letting the other get too far away from the other. They had not had their chance to talk as yet, but that would come. For now, Nickol needed to sit and then tell his story to their family and the friends who had gathered. Abe and Emma had appeared once more, this time with Jonathan and Frankie. Jonathan had not wanted to come, afraid that his presence would bring more danger to Nickol. He really hadn't been given a choice by Frankie, who simply stated that Nickol needed to know who had freed him.

Nevina found herself wrapped tightly in Nickol's arm as he sat on the love seat, more than willing to stay as close to him as she could. She was still deeply afraid, afraid that Nickol would disappear on her once more and never return to her or return to her just for her to plan a funeral. Her silent prayers begged God to keep her beloved groom safe.

Abe simply looked at the group and then bowed his head and began to pray. His prayer was picked up by the others in the room, who all understood the importance of their prayers.

John looked up as they finished, knowing that Nickol wanted to speak but was reluctant to.

"Nickol? How be you tell us what happened? You don't need a lot of details." John didn't take his eyes from his friend, seeing the understanding in Nickol's eyes of the out that John had just offered.

"Thanks, John. I can do that. At least, I think I can." Nickol rubbed at his temple, a headache beginning. "I'll just say what I can. Some things I can't say." He began to speak, simply stating what had happened, what he had felt, and how he had been rescued. His eyes were on Jonathan, not telling who had been the one who saved him but his gratitude showed to that man. "I know who it was." Nickol stated the name, seeing the understanding on his father's face and also on Trevor's. He could hear the murmurs around the room as the others took in who he had named.

"You're sure, I know, son." Niall spoke up at last, his voice bringing silence to the room. "So, now we need to prove it and also to prove if he's working on his own. I don't know that he would be. He doesn't have the smarts or the contacts."

"I don't think he is. He never spoke with me. I suspect that I was going to be made to work for him, helping in his poaching and whatever else that entailed. I couldn't do that." Nickol was sober as he spoke, having already spoken with his employer. That had been the consensus that they had come to.

Late that afternoon, John walked towards the front door, Nickol behind him. He was the last one of the group to leave. He had hesitated about staying, catching a look on Nickol's face that had him doing just that.

"Nickol? What didn't you say?" John knew his friend well enough to know that Nickol had not said everything that he could.

"I don't know, John. John Thompson took care of me the last few days. I know you know him. He and Mary were great, getting me back on my feet, finding Frankie for me to speak with, putting me in touch with Abe and Emma. There's just something missing in all this." Nickol sighed. "I can tell you who got me out, but I am afraid for his life." Nickol's lips snapped shut at that. He stopped near the top of the stairs on the front porch, an arm wrapping around a white-painted column.

John studied him before he nodded. He had wondered at Jonathan being there, not knowing the younger man. He had suspected at the time that Jonathan had had something to do with freeing Nickol. Nickol had confirmed that fact by not saying anything.

"I see, Nickol. Listen. You need to rest. I don't suspect that you or Nevina will be in church tomorrow. If you need me, call me." John's hand rested on his friend's shoulder as he prayed for him.

Nickol stood for a while, his face tilted to the fading sun, drawing in deep breaths of the fresh spring air. He felt an arm around him and simply wrapped Nevina close to him. He had been so afraid when he was a captive that she would be harmed or die or even move on from him. That hadn't happened. God had protected her. But now that he was home? He didn't know how to do that.

Chapter 21

A week later, Nevina moved through the woods once more, seeking for just the outdoor life photos that she needed. Nickol had not been happy that she was out there but she had a long-time client who had made a special request for her. As it was a Monday, Nickol was at work, this time in the office. It had been decided that for now he would work there unless he had to absolutely be out in the field and then he would only be out there with an officer accompanying him. He had not liked that but had agreed, knowing it was for the best.

Nevina hesitated as she heard a sound behind her and found somewhere she could hide. From her hidden spot, she watched the man following her footsteps and frowned. She didn't know him. He was not from one of the security teams, she knew that. She waited, barely breathing until he disappeared from view. Nevina's feet sped towards the parking lot and her vehicle. She was driving away as rapidly as she could even before she had completely fastened her seatbelt.

The man ran towards her, frustration on his face. He had been instructed to find her and bring her to his boss, the same man who had held Nickol as a captive. His thinking was that if he had Nevina in his control, then he could control Nickol. He didn't realize the characters of the couple and that they would never agree to his plans.

Nevina slammed the front door behind her, shoving home the locks before she stood, back to the door, her hand on her throat as she struggled to breathe. Someone had been out there, she knew, and had followed her, determined to bring harm to her or to Nickol. She wasn't sure which one it was. Nevina stared at the camera in her hand, afraid suddenly that she would need to give up the work that she loved and had only ever wanted to do.

Pacing through the house, she set her camera on her desk before she turned to study the office. Nevina nodded her head. Nickol had set up the both of them in the one room, simply stating that was how it would be. He wanted her near him. A kiss had followed his words as well as a deep hug. Nevina was in love with her guy and he with her. Only, she was so afraid that he would disappear once more on her or that she would disappear on him.

Hours latter, Nevina looked up as she heard the lock on the back door open and then Nickol's soft whistle. She stared at her watch, not realizing that she had been lost in her work, editing the photos that she had taken that morning and then sending them on to her client. She had immersed herself in research of the name that Nickol had provided, not really finding much at all.

On her feet, Nevina headed for the kitchen, frowning as she didn't find Nickol there. Instead, she headed for the bedroom, hearing the soft sounds of the shower through the closed door. She smiled. She had liked the solitude of her life at one point. But now?

Having Nickol in her life? That made her realize just how solitary her life had been.

Nickol paused as he stood in the ensuite doorway, his eyes on Nevina before he was across the room, wrapping her into a tight hug. His kiss found her mouth before his head laid against hers.

"Have a good day, love?" Nevina's voice was quiet, not wanting to disturb him.

"I did. It's hard being in the office but it's only fair right now." Nickol leaned back to look down at her. "And how about you? Get the pictures that you wanted?"

"I did and I have already sent them on to the client." She bit at her lower lip, a sign that Nickol recognized as her being troubled. "Someone followed me to the woods today, love. I didn't see much of him. I was able to hide and then escape. When will this be over? Does John even have any idea?"

"He hasn't said how far along in the investigation they are. It may be that they are waiting for some responses to come in." Nickol sighed. "Or it may be that it has gone cold and they have to wait for more information to come in."

"Or for something to happen to us." Nevina leaned harder against Nickol. "I'm scared, Nickol. I don't want anything to happen to you but there is always that possibility. Or to one of our family."

"That is true." He turned her to walk towards the kitchen. "I'm not very hungry. How about you?"

Nevina shook her head, reaching for the loaf of bread to butter some slices as Nickol reached for sandwich fixings in the fridge.

Late that night, Nickol stood at the living room window, the drapes partially open, and watched the vehicle that had parked in front of their house. Two men had exited the car and were walking towards the house. Nickol frowned as he didn't recognize them. He felt a hand on his back and then Nevina leaned against him.

"Who are they?" She kept her voice low.

"I don't know. Hopefully, they will appear on the security system and we can pass it on to John or Jerome." Nickol frowned before he was into the office, the security feed pulled up to watch. "No, they're some of Abe's men, I think. Joseph and Nathaniel. Why would they be here at night?"

"I have no idea." Nevina reached for her phone, frowning at the text message. "Abe sent them. Emma received word that we were to disappear tonight. They're not alone. Some of Don's and Richard's men are here as well. All we need is Peter and yes, she has reached out to him. He's away."

Nickol gave a low laugh even as he wrapped an arm around his lady. A kiss was dropped on her temple as he felt her leaning against him.

"We'll be okay, sweetheart. But you need to sleep. You can hardly keep your eyes open." He turned them towards the bedroom, finding Nevina just refusing to move that way. "Nevina?"

"It's okay. I'm going to make us coffee. I don't know that we'll sleep much tonight, not with the activity that's going on outside our home." She walked away, leaving him to watch her before he sighed.

Nevina was likely correct, Nickol decided, heading after her and finding the cookies that she had baked that day. He loaded a tray with their mugs of coffee and the plate of cookies, waiting for Nevina to walk towards the living room. He frowned as she hesitated for a moment.

"Nevina?" Nickol hesitated before he set the tray back down. He turned at a tap at the door, heading that way, peeking out to find Abe and Richard standing there, waiting for him to open the door. "Guys?"

"Pack a bag for yourselves, Nickol. We need to move you two out of here and now." Abe almost barked his commands at them, leaving Nevina running for the bedroom, returning with the bags that she had packed earlier without Nickol being aware of it. Abe gave a grim smile. "Prepared, I see."

"I am. God told me to. I have to listen to His voice. Where are we heading?" Nevina handed the bags to Richard and Don and then followed Abe, her hand tight in Nickol's, finding them surrounded by men, more than she could count in the dark.

Chapter 22

Later that night, Nickol paced the bedroom of the house that they had been rushed to. It was across town from his own place, hidden in the outskirts of town. He had never known it was there. His eyes found Nevina and a sad smile crossed his face. She had finally curled up under a blanket, sleeping but with tears on her face. Nickol dropped to his knees beside the bed, wrapping her into a hug and praying for her. He prayed for peace for both on them in the trouble that they found themselves in. He knew it was far from over.

A knock on the the door had him rousing and then rising to his feet. Nickol stared down at Nevina again before he bent, delivering a kiss to her cheek. He straightened up and walked to the door. A hand rested on the knob as he turned once more to study his bride.

Opening the door, he found Richard waiting for him, an unreadable look on his face.

"Richard?" Nickol followed him as the other man turned and walked away, heading for the kitchen. He took the mug of coffee offered to him before he found a seat at the table, studying the four men who sat there, all leaders of a security team, and well versed in the dangers that the couple faced.

"Nickol? We need to make some plans." Peter spoke for the group, knowing Nickol the best of them all. "Your families are safe. We have them somewhere no one will find them. And yes, Nigel did fight us on that." He gave a grin as Nickol snorted at that. "I know, Nickol. But it is necessary. Now, you two. What are we to do with you two?"

"I have no idea. I need to continue to work. So does Nevina. It's not an option for either one of us." Nickol was not backing down from the four. He was simply stating what was real for the couple.

"We understand that, Nickol." Don spoke up. "We'll work with you on that. I talked to your boss. He's fine with you in the office for now. If you need to be out and about, we have men with you. As for Nevina, the two ladies on Richard's team will be with her during the day. There will be some of the men from our teams around as well. We will do our utmost to protect you both."

"And unfortunately, you can do your best but it doesn't always work out the way that you hope, pray and plan." Nickol's head dropped for a moment in fatigue before he was on his feet and heading for the bedroom, stretching out beside Nevina and wrapping her into his arms before he too slept. He tried to pray but words would not form. Nickol knew that was when the Holy Sprit prayed for him.

Don had risen and moved to the doorway to watch Nickol walk away. His head dropped for a moment as the bedroom door closed softly before he turned back to the room. He reached for the coffee carafe and refilled their mugs, returning it to the element before he sat, his eyes closing for a moment.

———

Abe's head bowed as he began to pray, petitioning God for safety and peace for this young couple. He knew what it was like to face danger. His team had faced that as had Richard's and Don's. Abe in fact had been separated from Emma for ten years, after they had married just before graduating from university. He didn't want to see that happen to anyone else.

Richard paused as he finished their time of prayer, his usual "I love You' echoing in the room as he always ended his prayers. He looked up at last, assessing what they knew and what Emma and her team were finding as well as what John and his team were as well.

"Where do we stand?" Peter felt as if he was playing catch up, not having been there when the couple were moved.

"Not where we would want to be. Emma's having trouble finding what she needs to and that is not usual for her." Abe rubbed at his face. He was exhausted and knew everyone else was. "We need to end this and soon for them. They've seen what Slavin and Shaye and Roane and Ragen went through. They have heard our stories. How do we do this?"

"They won't stay away for long." Peter spoke again. "It's not them. They will want to make a stand and fight. We're just not ready for that to happen."

"They will and no, we're not." Richard sighed. "This is where it gets so dangerous. We know that feeling first hand."

"We do." Don thought back about his adventure with his now wife, Delanie. "We need to find the one responsible. How close are we to that?"

"Not where we need to be." Richard shook his head, his hand reaching for his pen. "What do we know or suspect?"

An hour later, he looked up and then was on his feet, heading for the outdoors. He needed to check in with the men who were out there. Two from each of their teams were around. No one felt that it was over kill. It was simply them trying to do their best to keep Nickol and Nevina alive. That their lives were in danger was not something anyone of them denied.

"Stephen?" Richard stopped beside one of his men, who was teamed up with Micah from Abe's team.

"So far, it's clear. But I'm not liking this, Richard. It doesn't feel safe. All of us are convinced of that." Stephen's eyes probed the darkness around them.

"It know. It's what we could do at the time. We're moving in the morning." Richard walked away, to do his own rounds of the property, stopping to speak with each of their men, and finding each of them shared Stephen's thought.

"Abe? Don? Peter?" Richard found the men still in the kitchen. "We're not safe here. All of our men are commenting on that. I think we need to move and move tonight."

"That's what we have just decided." Peter was on his feet, heading for the bedroom doorway and tapping slightly.

Nickol raised his head, rubbing at his eyes, before he rose and opened the door. He was not surprised to find Peter waiting for him.

"We're moving?" Nickol had thought that would happen.

"We are. And this time? You and Nevina move separately. We'll head out to somewhere else but not together. Get her up and then grab your belongings." Peter hesitated. "No, on second thought, don't. We need to go over them."

Nickol stared at him before his eyes slid closed. It was possible that someone had been in their home and set GPS trackers into their belongings. That had never crossed his mind.

Turning back, he roused Nevina, holding her as she wept for a moment before he set her on her feet and reached for her hand. He kissed her, not knowing when they would be together again but that they would be. That was a promise the four leaders had made to them.

Chapter 23

Nickol watched as Nevina walked away with Murphy and Stephen, one man from Abe's team and one from Richard's. This was how it had been explained to them. They were being separated just until they could reach somewhere of safety. He knew that one of Don's men, Caleb, he thought was behind the wheel of the car. Nickol sighed to himself before he turned, finding Ian from Abe's team, Paul from Don's team, and Timothy from Richard's team waiting for him. He hesitated, feeling a sense of evil and doom approaching.

"We need to get out of here, Nickol, and now." Paul shoved him into a truck before he jumped in after him, watching as Timothy drove away. He sighed. He saw the vehicles approaching. His phone was out as he sent a text message off to Don and then tucked his phone away.

"Someone's out there?" Nickol phrased his words as a question even though he knew the truth.

"There is. We just made it out in time." Paul nodded at the other two men. "We'll find our teams and your bride, Nickol. It will just take us some time."

Abe strode through the new house that they had found, outside of Nickol's town but still in that jurisdiction for law enforcement. John had appeared, watching as the teams set up their surveillance.

"When will they be here?" John had an idea that the timing would not be exact.

"Should be shortly." Richard paced. This was when it was always difficult, coordinating the care of their protected persons and keeping everyone safe and alive. He turned as he heard a truck, frowning. "Timothy's here? Where're the others?"

The four team leaders shared a look before the three with members out there were trying to reach them.

"I can't reach them." Abe was angry and afraid. "We need to start searching. John?"

"On it. Give me a description of the vehicle, the plate number, and who all was there." John took the proffered piece of paper and walked away, not stopping as Nickol passed him.

Nickol stared at the grim look on the men's faces and his eyes closed. Nevina was not here and that meant she was in danger.

"Where are they? Where's Nevina?" He spun as he stared at each man before he turned to run for the door, stopped in his tracks for Mark and Micah. "I need to find her."

"We know." Mark, from Don's team, just kept a hand on Nickol's shoulder. "We can't have you out there, Nickol. This is what they are waiting for."

Nickol's head went back as he stared up at the ceiling before he abruptly turned and walked back to the kitchen. A hand reached to pull out of chair that he sank into, his head cradled on his arms folded on the tabletop. The men moved around him on almost silent feet, their voices quiet as they spoke.

John stood by his car before he was in it. A car matching the description that he had been given had been found. There were three men there, unconscious, but no sign of a lady. That worried him to no end. Had Nevina disappeared once more?

John watched as Murphy, Timothy, and Caleb were assessed and then loaded into ambulances to be transported to the hospital. Murphy had roused to some degree, a hand up to beckon for John.

"We tried, John. We sent Nevina to hide when we were overwhelmed. She ran that way." Murphy pointed away from them, towards the woods. "I'm not sure if she was able to hide. They were waiting for us, and I would like to know how. The only ones who knew where we were with our teams. And they would not tell anyone." Murphy slipped back into unconscious, the gas that they had been hit with doing that.

John had stepped back, his eyes on the scene and the teams moving around it and then turning to walk towards the woods. He was careful to stay to one side, knowing that he had to. He sighed. Nevina had disappeared and with night coming, it would be difficult to search for her.

"John?" Edward stood beside him. He had been on duty when the call had come in. He was desperate to make the empty spot on the detective team and was doing everything that he could to do that. "Jerome's here."

"Thanks, Edward." John bit at his lip. "We'll need to search but our K-9 officers are tied up."

"I know someone. Bradon from the Barnabas Foundation. He trains dogs for security and search and rescue. Barnabas from there reached out. He simply said that Bradon was on his way here with his dog, Kade. How did he know?" Edward was puzzled by that.

John gave a short bark of laughter before he sobered. It was not the first time that Barnabas had reached out that way.

"He tells me that God directs him. Did you know that twelve of the men working for him are orphans and from across the country? God directed him to them. And they share initials." John grinned slightly as Edward stared at him. "And they have all undergone adventures as they term it, including Barnabas."

Edward shook his head as he watched Jerome walk towards them, a man and a dog walking beside him.

"Is that Bradon as you called him?" Edward pointed towards them.

"It is. Bradon? Good to see you even under these circumstances." John hesitated before he spoke. "Murphy said they sent Nevina that way. It's dark enough that I can't see her trail."

Bradon nodded. It was not the first time that he had searched in the dark.

"No one has walked after her?" He thought someone would have at least to see if they could find her.

"Not yet. Not that we know of. I've managed to keep anyone off to the side of where we think the trail is." John was not hopeful that Bradon and Kade, a beautiful Australian Shepherd, would be able to find Nevina.

"I see. Let me walk through what I can tonight. And then I'll be out here as early as I can tomorrow morning. You have people to go with me?"

Jerome nodded. He had far too many volunteers.

"Edward here will go with you. The four security teams are sorting out who to send with you. I think Richard is sending either Silver or Naomi just to have a female member with you."

Bradon nodded. He knew the three teams fairly well, Peter's not as much. It was exactly what he had expected to have happen.

Chapter 24

When Murphy had shoved Nevina from the car and then towards the woods, she had hesitated until she heard the fierceness of his voice, ordering her to run and find somewhere to hide. Her life depended on it. She ran, hearing the men's shouts behind her. Her feet picked up their pace as she reached the edge of the woods. Nevina had hesitated for a moment, vaguely recognizing the area. It was one that she frequented to find her photos but she had never ventured too far into the darkness of the forest. Today, that would change. Her life depended on it.

Nevina paused for a moment, a hand over her open mouth to hush the harshness of her breathing, as she stared around and then behind her. She had no idea where she was or how far she had ran. Time and distance had meant nothing to her. And that was now something that she had to deal with.

Hearing the sound of footsteps near her, Nevina sank back behind some bushes. She frowned, a headache starting behind her eyes. The sound was not that of a man but of a woman. But what woman would be out here? Her eyes closed for a moment even as she fought against the tears that just had to start. Unable to prayer coherently, Nevina begged God to protect Nickol and the men who had been with her. She feared for their lives.

A hand on her shoulder had Nevina stifling a yell before she looked up, frowning at the woman standing there. The woman's face was lined with hard work, worry, and loss of hope, her eyes gentle even through all that. Her clothes were worn, stained, faded, and patched in many places. A work-worn hand lifted Nevina to her feet.

Stumbling as she walked away with the woman, Nevina had trouble as she put one foot down and then the other. She was fatigued beyond what she had ever experienced. Without a doubt, she had inhaled some of the same gas as the men, but not enough that it had her losing consciousness. She just followed the woman, not knowing if she was heading into deeper trouble or to safety.

The woman turned at last, staring at Nevina, even as her hands found the bar to drop across the door. The same hands, in a gentle manner, directed Nevina to a rough bunk where she was forced to lie down before worn yet clean blankets were pulled over here.

Nevina slept, feeling safe for the time being, but not knowing who the woman was or if she was truly safe.

The woman, Anna by name, watched Nevina before she reached to set the kettle on the wood stove to heat. She had no running water, hauling in what she needed and heating it. Her cabin was rough but clean and tidy. She worked hard to keep it that way. Hers was a lonely life, broken only when her nephew would appear. She dreaded when he came. He was into evil and crime and didn't think twice about destroying something in her home that he didn't like.

Anna stepped back after washing what she could of Nevina's face and hands. She was worried about the young lady. Her finger touched the wedding band and engagement ring. Some man out there was missing her. If her nephew appeared and this lady was still here, this lady would never go back to her family. He would see to that. It would not be the first time that he had bragged of just that. And Anna knew in her heart that she could not be part of it. She hadn't been in the past, not knowing about the young ladies until it was too late and he had buried them where their families could never find them.

Twelve hours later, Nevina still slept. Anna had managed to rouse her enough to help her get cleaned up to some extent and some broth into her before Nevina slept again. It was as if she had given up. Anna was afraid of just that.

Anna turned as she heard a soft sound from outside her cabin and then crept to the window by the door. She stood to the side, watching the men who searched around her clearing before she heard a tap at the door. She was frightened but the men didn't seem to mean her any harm. She slid back the bar, holding it in such a way that if she slammed the door shut it would slid back into place.

"Can I help you?" Her voice had the man turning back to her.

Abe smiled at the lady in front of him. They were confident that Bradon and Kade had tracked Nevina to this cabin. He just had to confirm that and then remove Nevina to safety. And he would not be leaving this lady behind him. Of that, Abe had already determined.

"Good morning. My name is Abe Finlay. We have tracked a friend to here. A lady by the name of Nevina. Do you have her safe?" Abe continued to smile, not stepping forward at all, allowing Anna to determine if and when he did that.

Anna studied him, not sensing that he meant her any harm. She then turned her attention to the men in her clearing, milling around but on guard, it seemed. She was not afraid of them, turning back to Abe.

"Come in." She watched him closely as he stepped into the cabin, another man with him.

"This is the paramedic that I work with, Matt. He would like to examine Nevina if she's here." Abe once more waited patiently for Anna to speak or move.

Anna breathed a prayer for Nevina, not for herself. She had given up on herself years ago, resigned to the fact that she would never leave the clearing or her cabin.

"Over there. On the bunk. She's been asleep except for a bit ago when I could rouse her. I don't know what's wrong." Anna wrapped her arms around herself as she watched Matt kneel beside the bunk and begin his assessment.

Abe didn't move from where he stood by the door but he had assessed the one-room cabin and then Anna. There would be no way that he would let her stay there, not when word got out that she had helped

Nevina. She would likely lose her life over that and he couldn't allow that to happen on his watch.

Matt walked slowly back to stand beside Abe, a frown momentarily on his face.

"I would say that she inhaled some of the gas that got Murphy and the others but it's as if she's giving up." Matt knew that feeling. He and his now wife, Sarah, had felt the same way at times during their adventure.

"I see. We need to move, Matt, and now." Abe turned to Anna, a gentle smile on his face once more. "Anna, you've told me your name. I would like to repay you for helping our friend. Come with us. We'll find somewhere you can stay and live. I have a friend who will help you at no charge."

Anna stared at him, not sure at first whether to believe him or not. When she read correctly that he was offering her a way out, her eyes closed before she was moving around the cabin, gathering up just what she needed. She had planned that over the years, determining just what she would take with her.

Matt had gathered Nevina into his arms and walked away, heading out on the trail back to civilization surrounded by some of the men. The others, including Bradon and Kade, had waited for Abe. They surrounded Abe and Anna, walking them rapidly from the cabin.

None of them saw the young man, decrepit in dress and manner, who stumbled into the clearing thirty minutes after they left, yelling loudly with an alcohol-soaked voice for his aunt. He was astounded that she was not there. She always was. He began systemically destroying the cabin, finally setting it ablaze, standing back and watching it burn to the ground. He gave an evil cackle, thinking that he had destroyed his aunt's life, not realizing that she had moved on that day and would not be back.

Chapter 25

Cradling Nevina carefully in his arms, Matt walked carefully forwarded, surrounded as much as possible by the men with him. Bradon and Kade kept step with him, both alert to any danger around them. Abe followed with Anna, a hand out at times to steady her. He frowned for a moment, not sure who she was but she seemed familiar to him. As to why that was, he wasn't sure. He pulled out his phone and sent off a text to Emma, asking her to look into Anna.

Anna stared at the men around her, feeling safe for the first time in years. She had always feared her nephew, knowing the black heart that he had. She wondered just what all he was involved in and didn't know if she wanted to find out.

"Anna? You're all alone?" The man next to her, Richard by name he told her with a smile, questioned her.

"I am. I have a nephew that I try to avoid." She sighed. "You'll need his name. I don't know what all he is involved with. I was so worried about that young lady. If he had appeared when we were alone, she would have disappeared. It wouldn't have mattered to him that she was married. I know that he has killed young ladies before and buried them where they can't be found. Can you look into that?" Anna looked up at Richard, amazed at his height.

"We can, Anna. That we can do. We have friends who will help. In fact, Abe's wife runs a business where she finds people and information. She will work on that for you." Richard's hand went out to steady her as her steps faltered.

"Oh, she can't do that. I don't have any money. I barely could afford what little food I had to buy." Anna's voice broke with the sobs that she was trying to control.

"Anna?" Abe waited as her steps paused and stopped before she looked at him. "There is no charge. It's what Emma does. We consider you a friend. You helped a friend of ours and it's our turn to repay that." Abe smiled at her, bringing relief to her heart. "She'll want to meet you, that much I know. And we have friends who will help you get set up in a house or an apartment at no charge to you."

"You do?" Anna's feet started to move again as she thought through what they had said. "It's being God's hands and feet on earth."

Abe and Richard shared a look over Anna's head. She had put into words what they did.

Nickol turned from his desk at work. He had not wanted to be there but had to work. He rose, walking from his office and through the building, knowing that some of the security team were around. He paused as he saw Abe walking towards him, determination in his steps.

"Abe?"

Nickol's voice had Abe raising his head before he reached out a hand to rest on Nickol's shoulder. He knew that Nickol would run for a vehicle and take off on them unless he was kept in place.

"We have Nevina, Nickol." Abe's hand tightened on Nickol's shoulder. "She's at the hospital. We're here to take you there, if you can leave." Abe looked past him at Nickol's employer, Erik, who nodded at the question on Abe's face. "Come on, then. Let's get you to her."

+Okay.' Nickol hesitated, not sure whether to believe Abe or not. He felt Erik's arm across his shoulder and heard his prayer for him.

"Off you go, Nickol. We'll put away your work. Take what time you need." Erik watched Nickol walk away, his work mates surrounding their boss. "Nevina's home but Abe didn't say much."

"No, he wouldn't." Geoff walked away, not sure where to go. He stood in Nickol's office before he carefully locked away what needed to be. He handed the keys to Erik, knowing that Nickol would not be back that day or even the next.

Nickol paced the waiting room at the Emergency Department at the hospital. Nigel paced beside his brother, not willing to let him walk on his own. Niall watched his sons, an arm around his wife. They were sober as they watched the two, Niall tracing through the years as the boys as he called them had grown from newborns to curious children to responsible teens and then dedicated adults, strong in their faith in God and in one another. The boys had had their differences over the years but nothing that they had not been able to pray through.

Nickol hit the outside door and then paced the parking lot, Nigel still at his side. He didn't realize that Slavin and Roane had appeared, called to come by Ami, who knew that her son needed his friends who had gone through danger.

Looking around at last, Nickol's footsteps slowed before he stopped. He didn't realize that so many had come to just be with him. Tears blinded him for a moment as Nigel hugged his brother, holding on for longer than normal. Nigel stepped back and watched as their friends moved in to do the same, police officers standing with their backs to the group, on guard for what may or may not happen.

"Any word, Nickol?" Slavin stood with his hands on Nickol's shoulders, not letting him move away from him.

"Not yet. They told me it would be a while." Nickol blinked to clear his eyes once more. "I just want to know why." He looked up as Murphy and Abe appeared in his line of sight. He had been certain that they had gone home. "Abe? Murphy?"

"We don't know anything more than yesterday. I'm sorry, Nickol. I'm sorry that we couldn't stop whoever it was." Murphy looked down, contrition in his voice and on his face.

"It's not your fault, Murphy. You three did what you could. Whoever this is was? He or she is well prepared." Nickol shared a look with Nigel and then with Slavin and Roane. He had a good idea who it was and it wasn't someone that anyone would have expected. He said the name of the man, seeing Nigel and his friends nod, John, Peter, Jerome, and Edward nodding as well. He hadn't been aware that they had approached him.

"Him?" Abe sighed. Emma was right once more. She had come across thoatname a few years ago and had been adamant that he was involved in crime. She just didn't have the information that she needed at the time. Now, she would be like a terrier with a bone, he told her, determined to prove that was true.

Chapter 26

Walking away from his family and following the nurse who had appeared to find him, Nickol prayed for his bride. He had no idea what Nevina had been through or why. Abe had spoken at length with him, Niall and Nigel flanking him as they talked, just bringing him up to date on what they had found. Abe went into more detail than he normally would have, knowing Nickol would accept nothing less than that. Nickol had been dismayed, to put it mildly, at what Abe and the other men had found. He had begun to pray more fervently for his lady, begging God to protect her and keep her safe. He knew in his heart that God was doing just that. It was just that he wasn't seeing that and that worried and scared him.

Pausing in the room doorway, Nickol's head dropped for a moment as he continued to beg for healing for his Nevina. He thought back for a moment over the years that they had been friends. He knew in his heart that he had planned at some point to ask her out on a date, that she was the only lady for him. Nickol had been afraid to do that, afraid that he would destroy their friendship and that he had not wanted to lose. Instead, circumstances had forced them to marry and he was deeply in love with his bride as she was with him.

Walking towards the bed, Nickol still hesitated. He studied the equipment around her and sighed. At least, she was breathing on her own, he decided that was good. His eyes traced the intravenous line that ran to her one hand before his hand reached to touch her face, before he bent to kiss her. He heard her soft sigh and felt her turn into his touch.

The physician hesitated for a moment, his eyes on the couple, before he walked forward to once more assess Nevina. He didn't understand why she was still unconscious. There was nothing that would lead him to suspect that she should be.

"Doc?" Nickol's voice brought his eyes to the younger man. "What can you tell me?"

"What can I tell you, young man? Not a lot. There is no reason for your wife to not be waking up. From what we can determine, she received a small portion of the gas yesterday but she ran. Whatever she went through during that time and when she was found? We don't know. She was fortunate that the older lady found her and kept her safe. Now, once she awakens, she can go home. I just can't tell you when. There are no injuries that need to heal. She will likely need counselling of some kind. I have names that I can give you." He frowned as Nickol gave a half smile and shook his head. "You don't think that she will?"

"Not that, Doc. It's just that we have friends we can talk to. Far too many." Nickol's attention went back to Nevina, not seeing the nod that the physician gave. He had been warned about that.

Awakening in the early morning hours, Nevina's eyes opened and she stared around, wondering that she was in a hospital room and not sure how that had happened. She was not remembering a lot, she decided, and needed to. She yawned before her head turned and her nose hit a solid mass. Nevina's head raised as she stared at the body lying beside her, realizing at last that it was Nickol. She gave a small smile and just cuddled closer to him, feeling safe at the moment wrapped in his arms. She didn't hear the nurse come in on her rounds. She just slept, content to be with Nickol and knowing that God was in control of what was happening.

A few hours later, Nevina slipped from the bed, searching for her clothes and then rapidly dressing. She exited the small bathroom to find John pacing the room, his eyes on her as she approached him.

"John? You need to talk with me?"

John nodded, before he pointed towards the room door. He walked out after Nevina, a hand on her arm to direct her to the waiting room and a chair where she could see her room.

"Talk to me, Nevina. What happened?" John's pad of paper and pen were out, not sure if he would need them.

Nevina shrugged. She frowned at him as she tried hard to remember and just couldn't.

"I don't know, John. I really don't. I remember us being at home and then told that we needed to leave. I don't remember much after that. I think I can remember running through some woods but even that seems more a dream than anything else." She sighed. "And you need me to remember."

"We do. Do you remember a lady looking after you?"

Nevina shook her head, turning it as she heard soft footsteps. She didn't recognize the lady who walked towards her, accompanied by her parents.

"Dad? Mom?" She was on her feet to hug them before she stopped in front of the lady. "Do I know you?"

"No, I don't think that you remember me. My name is Anna. I found you and brought you to safety. Friends of yours found us and brought us to safety. And it's a good thing I hear that they did. Your friend there went back to my cabin and found that it had been burnt down." Anna drew in a deep breath. "It would have been my nephew. You would not have come back to your husband or your family had he found you." Anna blinked away tears, not expecting Nevina to reach to hug her and then whisper a prayer in her ear.

"You need to stay here, Anna. Have you somewhere to stay?" Nevina felt a beloved arm come around her and leaned on Nickol.

"She does, Nevina. Barnabas and Breck are here, wanting to talk with us. They have an apartment that they arranged for Anna to have, rent free for as long as she needs it as well as support for her." It was their friends did, using the billions of the Barnabas Foundation monies to be the hands and feet of God on earth.

"That they have, Nevina." Anna blinked. She had begged God for a chance to escape the life that she had been forced to live, hiding in the woods, afraid to venture out too often because of her nephew and his vile threats towards her.

"And we have your nephew in custody, Anna." John had approached. "We found him yesterday when we went back out to your place. He was still there." John didn't continue and state how violent that man had become, causing harm to the officers arresting him. John had walked around the burnt cabin, sorrow on his face for the lady who had lived there. He could only pray that they would be able to reach her and free her with God's help from the bonds that had held her for so long. "And we have people who will speak with you. At no charge." He reached to hug the older lady before he walked away, leaving her speechless and in tears as she watched him do just that.

Chapter 27

Nevina walked through their home, refreshed from the long, hot shower that she had just had. She knew that Nickol was around somewhere, likely in the kitchen fixing them a meal. She hesitated as she watched him before he sensed that she was there and turned, his arms opening as she flung herself into them, sobs shaking her body.

Nickol swept his lady into his arms and headed for his chair in the living room, sitting and then just holding Nevina as she wept. He knew that it wasn't just from the day before but was from everything that they were going through. He had spent the night when Nevina was missing doing just that, weeping before his Abba Father and then waiting for the peace that only God could give. He had found it that night but he still struggled with keeping it uppermost in his mind. That took work, he decided.

"Nevina? Sweetheart?" Nickol tightened his hold on his lady, a kiss dropped on her hair.

"Nickol? I don't get it. Why? The guys are okay?" She felt his nod against her head. "I was so afraid when I woke in the night and didn't know for a moment where I was. I was so afraid that they were dead."

"No, they were gassed. You caught some of it but we don't know exactly what happened to you. I don't know that we ever will. You've blocked that." Nickol waited for Nevina to respond. When she didn't, he tilted his head to watch her. "Dad and your Dad talked to me when we were waiting for the doctors to assess you. They think that you have buried whatever it was really deep and that you may never bring it up again. I don't want that for you. I want you to deal with it. But God is in control. He protected you and brought Anna to find you. He brought Abe and the other guys in at the right time to find you two and bring you to safety."

"How did they find me? No one has said." Nevina shifted how she was sitting, her head going down against Nickol.

"Bradon and Kade. John reached out to them. I think we've talked with the guys from the Barnabas Foundation at a conference or two. Bradon trains security dogs and also dogs for search and rescue. Kade tracked you to Anna's cabin." Nickol didn't quite know how to proceed.

"They found us in time is what you're not saying." Nevina sighed. "God is working through this. I know that He is. He's protecting us, teaching us, leading us, and helping us to show His love and compassion to others." Nevina sighed once more. "I could have done without this, you know." Her voice was grumpy as she spoke, causing Nickol to grin before he gave a soft laugh. She poked him. "It's not funny, buster."

"No, it's not but that is just so you. Welcome home, sweetheart." Nickol reached to kiss her, moved back, and then moved in to kiss her again. "You need to eat."

"No, I don't think so. What all information has been left?" Nevina moved to rise, finding Nickol just tightening his hold on her. "Nickol?"

"Not at the moment, sweetheart. You're under orders to rest for today and I intent to see that you do. I'm off work for the rest of the week. You need me here." Nickol waited for Nevina to respond before he realized that she had drifted off to sleep, feeling safe and protected in his arms.

Two hours later, Nickol roused from his thoughts. They had been dark at times and those he had had to surrender to his Abba Father. He studied Nevina before he was on his feet, heading for their bedroom to tuck her under the blankets. He kissed her cheek and then walked away, heading for the kitchen. A tap at the door had Nickol heading that way instead. He stood for a moment where he could not be seen, studying the men who waited outside for him to answer the door. His head dropped. There would be no rest today, he could see that.

Opening the door, Nickol greeted each of the ten men as they moved past him. One from each of the security teams, he could see, as well as Breck and Barnabas. He was not surprised to seek Blackie and Simon from Mistletoe there as well. Frankie greeted him as did Bill from Elmton. These two held up bags that contained food. It was well known that they never appeared to visit someone without bringing food. As police officers, they understood that sometimes physical needs met led to information being shared.

Paul from Don't team looked around before he stopped beside Nickol.

"Nevina?"

"She's sleeping and has been for a while." Nickol sighed. "I don't know how to help her, Paul, other than to hold her and love her and pray for her."

Paul nodded. He had been through an adventure with his wife, Peyton, as had the others gathered here, other than Tony from Peter's team. Some of their adventures as they termed them had been more life threatening than the others.

"That's all you can do for now. We're here to work with you but more importantly, we're here to pray for you and for Nevina. I understand that some of our wives will be reaching out to her. Baird's Berneen is particularly eager to speak with her as is Brennen's Jaxcy. You know their story, that they married to save one another."

"I do know their story. I have been talking about them to Nevina. She recognizes them but had never heard their stories. That will help, I think." Nickol looked around as the men finished preparing their meal. "Thank you, guys. You have no idea how much this means."

"We do, to a certain extent, Nickol." Barnabas spoke for the group. "We can't fully understand what it is that you are going through. But we want to show our support, to pray with you and then to work through what you have. We've all done that. My guys are meeting in the evenings for a couple of hours at a time, working through what they can." He grinned suddenly. "Burnie wants to meet with you two. He thinks that what you're going through is familiar, as in a story line." Burnie was an mystery novel author and thought differently than the others.

The men laughed at that, not seeing Nevina appearing in the doorway before she found Nickol and was wrapped tight to him.

"Nickol? We've been invaded?" Nevina's quiet question broke through the stillness that followed the laughter.

"We have, sweetheart, in a good way. They're here to help us. And their wives want to meet with you." Nickol simply held his lady and waited for her to speak.

The men had turned, assessing the couple in front of them before sharing looks.

Breck approached Nevina, watching her closely. He could see the peace that she was finding, a peace that only God could provide. He nodded. Neasa, his wife, was correct in her assessment.

"Nevina? My wife, Neasa, has asked if she could call you or come and visit you. She would like to share and pray with you. We have a couple of friends as well who were forced to marry, both to keep one another alive. Berneen and Jaxcy would like to visit you as well." Breck didn't push it. He didn't have to. He saw the interest and hope on Nevina's face.

"I would like that. It's feel isolating to think you are on your own. I mean, I know that Nickol and I are walking through this together. But to hear from others who have faced something Iike this and to hear how God worked in their lives? We need to do that."

Nevina bit at her lip. "I just don't know where we would meet."

"How about at the Foundation building? We have lots of room for whoever it is that wants to come." Breck was second in command to Barnabas in the Foundation and had no hesitation to offer that.

"That would work. I think." Nevina groaned as she heard the soft laughter and saw the smiles on the faces. "That's not quite how I wanted to word that. For now? What are we up to? Can we solve this today?

That evening, Nevina set aside the concise summary of what they had discovered to one side. Simon had been responsible for that. As a former military police officer, civilian police officer, and now a private investigator working for Blackie's father, he had taken what they had found, thought, surmised, and whatever else he termed it and written it out for them all. Nevina had been surprised by the consensus that had emerged. She had also been surprised at the folder handed to her by Frankie, who simply said a friend who was a former forensics psychologist, had done a profile for them. Darci had felt that they needed to see it that day. She and her husband, Doug, Riverville's lead ETF officer, were planning on coming to see Nickol and Nevina in the next few days, if that was agreeable. Nevina had shared a look with Nickol who had simply nodded. He was more familiar with the people that were being mentioned than she was. Nevina felt as if she had had her head buried in the sand for far too long. She had scowled at Nickol as he laughed at her just a few minutes earlier before he wrapped her into a hug and kissed her.

Nickol whistled as he worked on a light meal for them. Neither of them were hungry, he knew, but they had to eat. His hands stopped for a moment as he thought back over the day before he nodded. It had helped, he decided, even though at times the conversations had been intense and heated. Nevina has not known what to make of those conversations, simply staring at the men as they discussed their thoughts and findings.

A hand on his back had Nickol turning to wrap Nevina close to him. He loved that lady so much, he was afraid to lose her.

"Okay, sweetheart?"

"I think so. Did we really have that many in our home?" She leaned against him, a finger rubbing at a blue button on his shirt.

"We did. They'll do it over and over, if we want, with different men showing up. And I suspect that their ladies will be in touch with you, just to provide a feminine side to the adventure. They work on it in competition to the men." Nickol grinned as he remembered the words that had been spoken about the ladies and the agreement among the all that the ladies really did help sort out what they were confused about.

"Darci called earlier. She and Doug want to come by tomorrow. I told her it would be okay." Nevina yawned, a hand up to cover her mouth. "She wants to bring in some friends as well."

"As long as you're okay with that and don't overdo it." Nickol seated Nevina before he placed the meal on the table. Seating himself, he reached for her hand, a blessing asked over their meal and a prayer uttered for safety and peace.

Nevina ate away at her meal, not really thinking about what she was eating. Her thoughts were on the men that had been there earlier that day and what they had discovered.

"Did we really discover something, sweetheart?" Nevina didn't look up. Instead, her concentration was on the hand that covered hers.

"We did. They confirmed who we thought it was and found out more about his family. I never knew he had that number of relatives in town. They have not shown it at all." Nickol was frustrated by that. "Now, the task is to determine who all is involved."

"We'll get there. I don't think that a lot of them are." Nevina pushed away her empty plate. "John had an interesting question. He asked if we had ever suspected that man when we were in school together. He hadn't."

"No, I don't know that I had." Nickol's head tilted to watch Nevina. "You did?"

"I think so, now that I look back." Nevina blew out a breath. "He was always watching everyone else and not participating in normal activities. Think about it, Nickol. He was never into sports or any of the clubs that we had. He always disappeared as soon as class was over. When he was at a function, he was on the sidelines, watching and weighing everyone."

Nickol kept his eyes on her and his hand tight on hers. He thought back over the years when they were in school and sighed. He had to agree with her.

"You're right. It was there all along, wasn't it? Now, John has to prove it." He reached for a piece of paper and a pen, jotting down their thoughts. He stared at the written words, not sure where he was heading with them.

"Take a photo of that and send it on to Emma. Frankie will want a copy as will Simon and Blackie. Breck too, I think." Nevina's head dropped. "Just send it on to everyone. We might as well. They'll all want it."

NIckol began to laugh as he rose to clear away the remnants of their meal.. Nevina was on her feet, heading for the front door, having heard a soft tap. She stared at the couple standing there.

"I'm sorry. Do I know you?" She frowned as Nickol came up behind her, an arm around her.

"No, I don't know that you do. I'm Berneen and this is my husband, Baird. Breck and Barnabas said that they had spoken to you. I'm sorry for dropping in so unexpectedly, but we were in town. Do you mind?" Berneen was uncertain as to their reception.

"Come in. Have you eaten?" Nevina was worried that she didn't have a meal to serve them.

"We have. Thank you, Nevina. Don't go to any special trouble for us." Baird held up a box that he had in his hand. "We were through Riverville earlier today and picked up some goodies from the Irish Bakeshop there. Ryley and Dave are friends and did go through an adventure as well." He grinned at the snort that Nevina gave, Nickol openly laughing at his wife.

"What is it with you guys? Did everyone you know go through something?" Nevina walked away with Berneen, heading for the kitchen and the coffee that Nickol had set to brew.

Nickol continued to grin, shaking his head at Baird. He had spoken with Baird early that week, not sure where it would go. He had not expected to see that man in their home.

"Where's Darbi?"

"He's at home. Some studying that he had to do. Besides, he wanted to watch our little one. That made it easy for us to take off for the day. He enjoys being an uncle." Baird bit at his lip, a sign that he was uncertain. "I talked to Breck and Barnabas. They said that you had come up with a name."

"We have. Nevina has him pegged from when we were in school together. I don't know that we guys saw what she saw. Sometimes, she has such a perception about people that is almost scary." Nickol hesitated in the kitchen doorway, watching the two ladies laugh over something. "Our ladies are getting along, Baird."

"They are. God has prepared them for this. We don't like what we have to go through. I certainly didn't plan on being kidnapped, freed, and then beaten until Berneen agreed to marry me. And she never planned on being held as a captive for over two months." Baird's arm went around Berneen, his head nodding at the question on Nevina's face. "That's what happened, Nevina. That's the condensed version on how we met. And our minister at the time, Buckley, was taken captive when we were the second time and forced to marry us. If Berneen had not agreed, I would be dead."

Nevina's hand went to her mouth to stifle her exclamation of horror. She studied the couple, seeing how much in love that they were, before she leaned against Nickol.

"We need to talk, I guess, then. The living room, I think, Nickol. The office is tidy but I don't want to be in there right now." She turned away to set out the mugs and whatnot on the tray, stepping aside as Nickol reached for it, a kiss delivered to her cheek as he did so.

Chapter 29

Three days later, Nevina wandered around the back yard of their home, her eyes on the gardens. She and Nickol had spoken at length the night before about what they wanted to do. He had been content over the years just to let the gardens do what they wanted. Nevina had rented her home and had not put a lot of work into what few gardens there had been. Her mind raced with the possibilities.

She turned as she heard a throat clear, frowning at the couple who stood there. She sighed. Here, she thought that she was on her own, ready to get her hands dirty and now that had changed.

"Can I help you?" She walked towards them, amazed at the height of the man and the petiteness of the lady.

"I hope so. You're Nevina. Nickol told us we would find you outside more than likely." The man grinned at her. "I'm Brennen and this is Jaxcy. But we've interrupted you." Brennen was hesitant in his words.

"You have, but it's okay. I was just assessing what I wanted to do out here." Nevina turned as she heard a sound from Jaxcy. "Did I say something that I shouldn't have?"

"It's okay. I lead the work with the gardens at home. You have a lot of lovely beds. What are your thoughts?" Jaxcy linked an arm with Nevina and walked off with her, leaving Brennen shaking his head, turning as he heard someone beside him.

Nickol stood there. He had been in to work and was bluntly told to go home. He was on leave, didn't he know that? Erik had grinned at him, before handing him a pile of files and told to go through them at home.

"Brennen? You two are here?"

"We are. Breck spoke with us last night. He felt a real urgency that we come today. He didn't say why. But then, that's Breck." It was not the first time that Breck had sent one of the men or a couple on a search for someone.

"No, he's like that, isn't he? All of you who work for the foundation are." Nickol nodded towards the ladies. "I suspect that they'll be a while. Nevina has always loved her gardens although she didn't do much at her rental home. And I know that Jaxcy enjoys them more now that it's not a source of survival for her."

"She does. You're right when you say that. She had such a ramshackle cabin down east. And her main source of food was her garden. I am still amazed how God kept her sane and happy despite all that." Brennen took the mug of coffee and found a seat on the deck. "Tell me, Nickol. Just where does your investigation stand? Burnie was muttering about sending on material to you."

"He did do that. We got it last night but haven't really taken time to go through it. Nevina is still healing from whatever happened to her. I don't want to push her even though John is. She stares at him and then walks away, leaving him frustrated with her." Nickol grinned as he remembered the look on John's face from the night before.

"And she will do that, Nickol, until she is ready to face what happened or is forced to." Brennen sipped at his coffee, his eyes on the ladies. They had found a seat near the back of the yard and appeared to be deep in conversation. "Our ladies are getting on well."

"They are." Nickol sighed. "Nevina is distancing herself from her parents and from mine. We think it is a preservation technique, but it's not going to work, is it?"

Baird shook his head. He had seen it with others of his friends and their ladies.

"No, it won't. All you can do is be there for her and pray for her. I sense that peace is what you two are searching for."

"It is. Nevina seems to be finding that more than I am." Nickol stared down at the mug in his hands. "I don't know how to pray, to tell you the truth. I pray that this is over but I also have to pray that God's will be done. How do you reconcile the two, the good and the evil?" He looked up as he felt a hand on his and reached for Nevina's hand.

"It's hard, Nickol. Many times, we both doubted that God was there. I mean, we trusted Him completely and fully in what we were going through but it was hard. When Abe tracked down Jaxcy's parents on that island so far away from us, it was as if God had heard our complaints and provided something so wonderful for us. She thought that they were dead. They didn't quite know what to think. They're still working through some of the issues surrounding that." Brennen shared a look with Jaxcy, seeing the confidence that she had in him. "All of our guys and ladies are the same. They doubted, almost walked away from God, but kept trusting him. They were used by God to bring people to justice. You'll find that fact true if you speak with anyone who has gone through this."

"That's what Slavin and Shaye and Roane and Ragen tell us." Nevina wrapped an arm around Nickol's. "It's hard, you know, to trust in Someone you can't see. You feel that you need to be doing what has to be done on your own, but you are restrained from that."

"That's a good way to put it, Nevina, restrained." Jaxcy nodded as her thoughts tumbled over one another. "It's what I felt all those years without Mom and Dad. I wanted to flee from my home but didn't. I guess I was waiting for them to come home. I'm sure now that I knew somehow that they were still alive, despite what was told to me."

"I can see that happening, Jaxcy. Thank you. You have helped just by coming here today and sharing just that simple fact." Nevina gave a small smile. "But it's not just a small or simple fact, is it? God loves us that much that His Son died and rose again for us. He has never left us comfortless, sending the Holy Spirit to walk with us through everything. We need those reminders. As we age in our faith, we can take it for granted, can't we?"

"You have a preacher for a wife, Nickol." Brennen grinned at her. "We need those reminders. Buckley is good for doing that."

"You have material for us, don't you?" Nevina shook a finger at him. "I know that you do but this has been what we needed, more than any information you could hand us. Can we spend some time in prayer? And at some point, I want to come and meet the rest of your family."

"You can do that. Bruce, Barnabas' father, was asking about you two last night." Brennen's hands went up. "I can't tel you how he knows when something is going on but he tells us that God brings people to his mind that he needs to pray for urgently and earnestly and then he works from that to help them in any way that he can.

Chapter 30

Hitting the garage wall with his outstretched hands, Nickol shook his head. The unexpected assault had not been what he had been expecting when he walked around the building, heading for the door at the back of the garage to find the lawn more. His body hit the wall next as fists pounded at him. He finally sagged to the ground, his eyes closed against the pain that he felt. His only thought was to be glad that Nevina was away that day, out on a photo shoot and that she had off-duty officers with her.

Nevina set her camera bag down on her desk and turned, feeling grubby from being out in the woods that day. She frowned. Nickol was to have been at home but she had not seen him. She shrugged even as she rushed to shower and change her clothes. He had to be somewhere.

She searched the house and then around it, stopping to frown. Where was hie? His car was here but he wasn't. She drew in a deep breath. Something had happened to him. Nevina ran for her phone, calling John. Just getting his voice mail, she began to panic, spinning in fear as she heard a sound near her.

Nigel watched his sister-in-law, not sure why she was panicking as she was. A hand drew her to a seat on the back deck.

"Nevina?" Nigel crouched beside her. "What is going on?"

"Nickol! I can't find him. He doesn't answer his phone. His car is here but he's not. At least I don't think he is. He's not in the house or around it." Nevina's focus was on the garage and she was running that way before Nigel could stop her.

Rounding the building, Nevina slid to a halt as she saw the crumpled form near the building. She was on her knees beside Nickol, struggling to turn him over and hold him in her arms, even as tears flooded her cheeks and her voice could barely find its way out of her mouth as she called for him to awaken.

Nigel stood in shook as he saw Nickol's limp body before he was on his knees as well, reaching to assess his brother as best as he could. Hearing the sounds of sirens and then slamming doors, he ran for the front of the house, finding Edward heading towards him. That man had finally made the detective squad and was doing his best to solve this case.

"Nigel? Dispatch said that Nickol was missing?" Edward's hand stopped Nigel from running from him.

"He's behind the garage. He's hurt and unconscious. Nevina's with him." Nigel broke Edward's hold on his arm and ran back towards his brother. He didn't see the officers fanning out to investigate and search. All he cared about was getting help for Nickol.

Edward stood and watched as the paramedics worked over Nickol, his arm restraining Nevina from being in the midst of that. They had had a struggle to make her move away from Nickol so that the emergency personnel could take over his care.

John walked towards the ambulance, stopping just short of the door. A grim smile lit his face as he heard Nevina's adamant refusal to step away. He shook his head at the paramedic who shrugged before slamming the door shut and heading for the driver's seat.

Edward stopped himself beside John, not sure what to say or even think.

"What happened? Do you know?" John spoke at last, eyeing Edward.

"Not really. Nevina came home and then realized that Nickol should be home. She couldn't find him at first, Nigel said. He had come to ask Nickol some questions about something and found Nevina almost in a panic, totally unlike her. She realized that she hadn't searched near the garage and then found him. I don't know much more than that. Nigel couldn't say and Nevina's not talking to us." Edward gave a quick grin. "There was no way that she was letting him go without her. We had to hold her back when they were assessing her."

"She's like that. He's not just her groom. He's her lifeline right now." John turned in a circle. "Someone's watching us."

"They have been." Edward frowned, puzzled by something. "Nickol said that they haven't been receiving the parcels, the threats by text or email, the notes on their cars, the sense that they are being tracked all the time."

"That's what he said. That means someone is very close to him." John paled, a hand reaching out for Edward. "You're not working the scene?"

"No, Jerome picked it up. Why?" Edward strode away with John.

"We're heading for the hospital and then to the office. There's someone we're missing and I want to go back over all of the people in the case that we have listed. It's going to be a long time." John paused as his phone chimed, staring at the message from Emma. "And Emma has come through." He tilted the phone to show Edward.

"Him?"

"Him and that makes it more dangerous for those two. They won't believe us." John stared over at Edward for a moment even as he raced towards the hospital.

"They will. Nevina was muttering something about him the other day. I think she has never liked him." Edward stared down at his folded hands. "And I have to agree with her. I watched him over the years. He was never sincere with anything. He also hung around outside of school with the one that they named already."

"He did? And did we know that?" John parked, a hand hesitating on his seat belt. "Edward?"

"No, I don't know that you did. I'm not up on everything on the file so I can't tell you if he was named. If he wasn't, then we have work to do, don't we?"

Nevina sat in the waiting room, her focus on the door to the examination rooms. She didn't feel Trevor's around around her shoulders or Ruth's hand on hers. She didn't see Nigel crouch down in front of her and wrap her free hand around a bottle. She didn't see anything around her. Nevina was simply too focused on Nickol, wanting desperately to be with him and knowing that she couldn't, not at present. The physician had been adamant about that when he had sent her out of the area with Nigel, extracting a promise from Nigel to keep her out there. Nigel had nodded, knowing that he wanted to be where his brother was as well. Their parents were there, he knew, worried about Nickol but also about Nevina.

Chapter 31

John walked back towards the physician, seeing the busyness of the Emergency Department that day. He frowned. It was a clear, warm spring day and he would have thought that it would not have been so busy. He shrugged, knowing that was how it went.

"Doc Brown?" John stopped beside the man, a member of their church. "Nickol? What can you tell me?"

"Nickol?" Doc Brown turned to face John. "We're still waiting for imaging to be done. He's been beaten thoroughly, John. It almost killed him, do you understand that? A few more moments and we would not be having this conversation. And lying on the damp cold ground? That hasn't helped. I hope you know that." Doc was grumbling at that point, stating the obvious and they both knew it.

"I see. Injuries?" John's notepad was out as he made his notes.

"Broken ribs. Left arm is broken. He has a concussion. His jaw is badly bruised. We're waiting for another set of images and then we'll get Nevina and the family back." Doc turned towards the door to the waiting room. "Cheryl was out there to speak with her. She's shut down, I gather."

"She is, Doc. I can see that. We need her to find Nickol, as bad as it is. I'm just not sure that she'll understand what all you're having to tell her." John walked away at that, pausing at Nickol's bedside to pray for his friend. This assault had just upped the urgency of the investigation even though they had been working on it all along. There was just that one piece of information that was missing, and John had an idea that Edward was working an angle that he would share soon.

Nevina was on her feet, nudged there by her father, his arm still around her as they followed Cheryl back to the examination room where they waited for Doc Brown to appear. Nevina's hand rested on Nickol's, finding his slack under hers. Her cheek rested against his, feeling the end-of-day whiskers rough against her skin. Her warm salty tears fell on his face, as she wept, unable to stop herself. Nevina knew that someone was with her. She just didn't know or care who it was. All that mattered was the man in front of her, lying silent and hurt.

Doc Brown stood for a moment outside of the room, a chart in his hand, as he studied Nevina. He was a good friend of her parents, he and his wife, and had known Nevina all of her life. She had a streak of steel running through her, he knew, that not many people saw. If it failed her now, he didn't know how they would help her.

"Nevina?" Doc's quiet voice had Nevina jumping in fear before she looked at him, terror on her face for a moment.

"Doc? What's wrong with him? Why isn't he waking up? He should be." Nevina's words tumbled over one another, run together as her fear drove her ability to articulate away.

"He was beaten, Nevina." Doc's arm around the lady he considered another daughter. "Badly at that. He has a concussion as well as broken ribs and a broken arm. He was also on the damp cold ground for a while. We don't know how long, do we?"

Nevina hesitated before she shook her head. She could tell them what time that she found him. She couldn't tell him what time it happened. And Nigel had looked over the security feed. It had been tampered with, taken down in the morning, so that was no help. She knew that the investigators would be reaching out to their neighbours, to see what they could find out.

"When can I take him home?" Nevina's voice was barely audible. She bent over the bed once more, her arms around her groom, sobs shaking her body.

"Not until at least tomorrow, Nevina. Look. I'll be back around. We're trying to find a bed on the floor for him but they're in short supply." Doc walked away, not content that he had given Nevina the information that she needed. She just wasn't listening to him. Not that he could blame her, he decided.

Nigel hesitated in the doorway as he followed his parents into the room. There just seemed to be too many people in there. Nevina looked around and saw him, walking towards him and into his brother hug.

"Nevina?"

"I'm okay, Nigel. I know. I know. I shut down. I couldn't help it." She turned to watch their parents, Nigel's arm around her helping her to stand on her feet. "Doc says they'll keep him over night and then see. I want to take him home but I can't. Not tonight." She was sober as she spoke, not sure when Nickol would go home.

"We'll all help, Nevina. You are not on your own." He turned as he heard footsteps and saw a couple approaching them. "Do you know them?"

Nevina peeked around him and then walked towards hug the couple. She was not surprised to see Dr. John Thompson and his wife, Mary, there.

"What brings you two here?" Nevina turned back towards the room, anxious about Nickol.

"You two do. Doc Brown reached out to us. We're off for a few days and readily agreed to help you two out. That way, Nickol can go home sooner." John hugged Nevina again before he walked into the room, greeting her parents and being introduced to Nickol's parents and brother.

Mary wrapped an arm around Nevina. She and John had been part of the adventures of some of their young friends. This time, though, it seemed different.

"Nevina? What aren't you saying?" Mary waited patiently for Nevina to respond.

Nevina shrugged, not sure what to say. Her emotions were all over the place at the moment and she had no idea what to think, say, or even pray.

"I don't know, Mary. I really don't know." Nevina looked around, lost for the moment. "Are you sure?"

"We are. You need us and to tell you the truth, we need you. John's in the process of retiring from the hospital and setting up a private practice just to help in situations just like this."

"He is? Oh, that's wonderful." Nevina walked away from Mary towards Nickol, a hand on his cheek as he stirred. She ignored the others in the room, her focus solely on NIckol before he slipped back into that darkness that just would not let him go. Nevina begged God to release him from that, to let him awaken, but it just wasn't happening at the present time.

Chapter 32

It had been three days since Nevina had found Nickol crumpled on the ground by the garage. She paced the hospital room, her eyes flickering from the window to the door and then back to the bed. She sighed. This was not working. Her heart was breaking, her emotions shattering. She didn't want to go on if Nickol didn't awaken. None of the medical personnel had been able to tell her when that would happen. They couldn't. Only God knew when that would happen.

Nevina had sent their parents on their way that morning. They had appointments and meetings that they needed to be at. She refused John's offer of an officer to sit with her. She had also sent the security teams away. What Nevina didn't know was that the teams had not gone far. One from each of the teams was around at all times, taking shifts in how they did that. It was how they did things for friends. There were also off-duty officers around as well.

Mary and John were still there. They had looked at one another and decided that they needed to stay for this couple. Mary walked into the hospital room just as Nevina reached the breaking point. She simply hugged the younger lady, holding her as she wept for what she had lost and what she was facing.

"It's not fair, Mary." Nevina swiped at her tears. "It's not fair that someone else has this much control over our lives. We should have been able to make the decision ourselves to date and marry if that was what we wanted. That was taken from us."

"It was, love, but it is in God's will for you. If it hadn't been, it would not have happened. He has walked this path before you. And He is walking right beside you, even now. He knows the hurt and heartbreak that you are facing. He bottles your tears." Mary hugged her again before shoving her down into a chair and finding her own chair. Her head bowed as she prayed for her young friend.

"I get that, Mary." Nevina swiped at the tears on her face. "I just hate that Nickol is like this. It shouldn't be." She sighed. "I know. I'm questioning God, aren't I?"

"And He understands that you need to. Can you tell me where it says we can't? David questioned God. The disciples questioned Christ. Moses questioned if he was fit to lead the Israelites from Egypt. I am sure that Moses' mother questioned having to give up her son to Pharaoh's daughter. I would have. It's what we do with the questions and the answers that we get that matters." Mary kept her eyes on Nevina, seeing as she understood what Mary was saying.

"I guess I understood that in some form, Mary, but you havre made it clearer for me." Nevina sighed. "You and John have to head off soon, don't you?"

"No, we don't. You and Nickol need us for now. You are the first of the ones that we are helping with our new work. And Nickol will awaken. God has promised us that. It doesn't mean that you have to like what you're going through." Her head turned as the door opened and a young man appeared. "Can we help you?"

The man hesitated. He was a youth really, barely out of his teens if that. Nevina had turned, frowning at him before she was on her feet.

"Jeff? What are you doing here? Should you be?" She drew him into the room further, seeing Abe standing in the doorway. She frowned at Abe before her attention went back to Jeff.

"I need to, Nevina. You and Nickol have always helped us out, those of us who are teens. I can't let them hurt him any more." He looked down at an envelope that he was worrying in his hands before he shoved it at her. "Here. This will help. It's information that we've gathered, my friends and I. They are staying hidden but I had to come to find you. Now, I need to find some place to hide." Jeff jumped as he felt a hand on his shoulder and looked up in fear at Abe.

"It's okay, Jeff, is it?" At his nod, Abe continued. "I have some friends here who can help. They'll take you back to my home area. It's really secure. We'll hide you there for now." Abe nodded at Nevina and Mary before he walked away, a hand still on Jeff's shoulder and found Ian and Luke, sending them away with Jeff. He feared for the young man and prayed that they would be able to keep him safe. His head turned as he studied the door to the hospital room, knowing that Nevina would speak with him if she needed to.

Nevina sighed, staring down at the envelope. She needed to look at it, but didn't want to. She set it to one side, determined not to think about it. Mary watched her closely, seeing the fragility that Nevina was determined to hide.

On her feet, Nevina stood by the bed, a hand on Nickol's cheek. If her will could have awakened him, then he would be awake and on his feet. That wasn't happening as yet. It would come, she decided. She just wanted it then.

That afternoon, Nickol stirred once more, his eyes opening as he squinted around the room. He was disoriented, he decided. There was no way that he was in a hospital room. But he hurt, all over, and breathing was difficult. Feeling the tug on his hand, Nickol stared at the IV line, frowning at it. When did that happen? A soft sound to his left had him jumping and then staring that way, finding his father waiting for him to speak.

"Son? You're awake. Let me call the nurse." Niall's hand reached for the call button, hesitating as Nickol shook his head. "You don't want that?"

Nickol swallowed hard, trying to lubricate his throat. He sipped gratefully from the glass of water his father held to his lips.

"Dad? What happened? I don't remember." Nickol shoved at the bed, reaching to raise the head of it.

"You were assaulted behind your garage. We don't know how long you were there before Nevina found you. That was three days ago or so. How are you feeling?" Niall watched his son closely, knowing that he would try and hide how he truly felt.

"Not great, Dad. They must have really beaten me." Nickol looked around, not seeing the one person he wanted to. "Nevina?"

"Nevina? That lady?" At the scowl from his son, Niall grinned. "That lady who refused to leave you? The one who advocated loudly and long for you? We've finally been able to get her to go home long enough to shower and find some clean clothes. Your mom and hers had a hard time convincing her to leave. She told me that she was afraid that you would die or disappear on her if she did go." Niall pointed behind him at the door. "Those young men with the security teams are around. They're not letting very many people through and in here."

Nickol sighed, a small smile on his face as he thought of Nevina.

"That's what they do, Dad. That's how they protect people." Nickol slept, this time a normal sleep. He didn't hear the door open and Nevina appear once more, to be hugged by Niall as he informed her that yes, Nickol had been awake for a bit and was now sleeping.

Niall walked away, his own emotions in a turmoil. He didn't feel Nigel's hug until he heard his other son praying. They hugged one another, grateful to God that Nickol had survived his beating and that God would heal him.

Chapter 33

A week later, Nickol walked slowly through his work place. An arm was wrapped around his chest, trying to ease the pain but it wasn't working as well as he thought that it would. He sighed. He should still be at home but there was work that he needed to do, and that work had to be done at the office. Nickol sank into his desk chair, his eyes closing against the pain for a moment. He had had a long talk with John and Edward the day before and was dismayed that they had no further information on who had attacked him or why. That meant the investigation was slowing and would need to be set to one side.

Geoff had walked Nickol walk away from the group before he shook his head at Erik and then walked to fill mugs with coffee for the two of them. He set Nickol's on his desk and then found a seat in front of the desk, his eyes on his friend.

"Geoff? What do we know about the beavers?" Nickol went back to that investigation. It was still open.

"Not a lot. You've done everything that you can to solve it. The men disappeared or so it seems." Geoff leaned forward, plunking his mug down on the desk. "What if they are still around? Working in the deeper areas of the forest that we can't access readily? Is that possible?"

"It likely is." Nickol stared at his computer screen, not seeing the screensaver flicking across it. "And I don't know how we would ever find out." He looked up at a tap at his door and waved the two men in. "Aidan? Kaelen? You two are here? Geoff, you've met Aidan. Kaelen is a copter pilot." His words stopped as he stared at the two of them. "You're here for a reason."

"We are, Nickol. Your name has come up in an investigation that I have ongoing. I can't go into many details but I was sent to speak with you. Kaelen approached me this morning, concerned as well." Aidan simply bowed his head and prayed for his friend. He looked up. "You were discussing something. We didn't mean to intrude."

"We were." Nickol shared a look with Geoff. "We have an area that we would like to investigate but it is very difficult to reach by foot. By copter? That's another story." He grinned as Kaelen grinned back at him. "God sent you two today." He looked up as he heard a sound and found Erik standing in his office as well. "Erik?"

"That's who we need, Nickol. A copter pilot. And God has provided that. Aidan, I know that some of the forest is under your police jurisdiction. That particular area that we need to search is there. Nickol, go on. Take Geoff with you and go and search. Just stay out of trouble, okay?" Erik waved them away, watching as Geoff packed up supplies and then ran for Aidan's truck. Please, Lord, Erik begged, let them find some answers today and end this soon for Nickol. I fear for his very life.

Flying over the requested area, Kaelen kept just high enough that he would not be a ready target but low enough for the other men to search the area. Nickol pointed to an area.

"There, I think, Kaelen. There's a clearing that you can land in not too far away." Nickol turned to Geoff. "It's been disturbed, Geoff."

"It has been." Geoff reached for his pack as the copter landed. "Kaelen, you stay here. We shouldn't been too long."

The three men walked away, leaving Kaelen to watch them and then watch the area around him. If necessary, he would take off and hover over them. For now, he was content just to wait.

Nickol stared at the disturbed area, seeing the carcasses of the animal that had been killed. It sickened him to know that this had happened and what little the killers had wanted from the animals had been taken.

"Let's get our pictures, Nickol. We need to get out of here and fast." Geoff was already at work, taking what was needed, watching as Aidan took his own photos and made his notes.

"All set?" Nickol was uneasy, certain that if they remained much longer they would meet the same fate as the animal.s

"We are. Let's get out of here and then assess what we have. We can do that at our office." Geoff led them off, almost on a run, dodging tree branches and shrubs in his haste to find the copter.

Late that afternoon, Nickol turned from his desk, reaching out to shake Aidan's hand. Kaelen had disappeared earlier, having to fly out on a job.

"Thanks, Aidan. This has helped. You have what you need?"

"I do, Nickol. You need to watch your back. They'll come after you, to take you out. You've discovered something that you shouldn't have, and I'm not fully convinced that it's due to poaching or smuggling of animal parts." Aidan bit at his lip. "What can we do for you?"

"For now, you've done what you can. I'll keep in touch. And I will take care." Nickol looked around as he heard a sound and found Nevina running towards him. "Nevina?"

"It's okay. Nigel dropped me off. Aidan? I didn't know that you were here." Nevina reached to hug their friend.

"I was here on an investigation that Nickol is part of." He waved as he walked away, leaving Nevina scowling after him before Nickol kissed her.

"I'm all set to go home. Are you?" He grinned at her. "How be we stop at the diner for our dinner? We haven't done that for a few days."

"Okay, I guess. I'm worried, Nickol. Where are they? Why aren't we receiving the packages, letters, photos, and angry voice and text messages?" Nevina tucked a lock of hair behind her ear.

"We haven't been. Aidan asked me about that but didn't say much. John has approached me as well."

Nickol hesitated before he reached for her hand. "Let's pray, sweetheart, find our dinner, and then lock ourselves away for the night."

Nevina's scream pierced the busyness of the downtown air the next afternoon. She backed frantically away from the man who was approaching her. She knew him and knew that he lived on the wrong side of the line of right and wrong. Her scream had startled those around her. The men spun and then ran towards her, the women heading for shelter, the ones with children scurrying quickly to get their families to safety.

"No. Leave me alone. I won't go with you." Nevina batted at the man's hands, knowing that she wouldn't be able to escape if he ever caught her. She didn't see the men reached to restrain him, despite his struggles to escape. Instead, she found herself drawn into a local store, the door locked behind her. Nevina looked up, surprised to see Roane and Slavin there.

"Are you okay?" Roane spoke for the two men, Slavin standing at the door watching the activity outside.

"I don't know. How am I to know if I'm okay?" Nevina's comment was just so here the men had to laugh before they sobered. "Did they catch him?"

"They did, Nevina. Men moved in and stopped him. John's out there right now with other officers. He'll find us when he can." Roane turned back to her. "Do you know that man?"

"I do. So do you. It's Ed Caine. You know? The one who owns the local newspaper? The one who never has anything good to say about our police services or anyone who helps out those in need?" Nevina's scowl grew deeper. She just didn't know why he had chosen to try and take her that day.

"Him? I heard yesterday that the paper had folded and he had no work. He's blaming you?" Slavin paced around her. "You had nothing to do with that."

"Not that I know of." Nevina's eyes slid closed as she sighed once more. "His wife. Margaret. She left him last week. I saw her as she boarded a bus and spoke briefly with her. Not about what she was doing. Just about a meeting that she wouldn't be able to attend. She asked me to pass on her regrets to that group's leader. Is that why? He thinks that I helped her to escape?" Nevina jumped as she heard another voice beside her.

"That's part of it, Nevina." John's face was grim. "He thinks that you helped her to arrange to get away. But there is something about some photos that you took a month ago. Do you remember that?"

Nevina was shaking her head. She hadn't taken any photos for him.

"Not that I know of. I would need more specifics as to what you mean." Nevina sighed once more. Her day had just changed. "And you want to go through my photos."

"I will. You were down here for a reason. Let Roane and Slavin help you and then get you home. I'll be by later. And yes, Nickol will need to hear what happened today." John walked away, needing to be somewhere else even though he felt strongly that she was still in grave danger. He also knew that two police officers were stationed outside of that store and would accompany her home.

Nickol turned as he heard the front door close and the lock engage. He stepped to where he could see Nevina, not liking the look that she had on her face. He paced towards her, wrapping her into his arms, feeling her jump as he did so.

"Nevina? Sweetheart?" Nickol waited impatiently for her to speak. "What happened?"

"What happened? I was downtown, just minding my own business. I needed some supplies and had headed for Joe's store. Ed Caine approached me and tried to kidnap me. The men who were around me saved me. Roane and Slavin were there too. I don't know where they came from." She looked up at Nickol, seeing the anger on his face. "John arrested him. He seems to think that Caine blames me for his wife leaving him."

"And you had nothing to do with that. You did mention that she asked you to pass on a message for her. Is that what he thinks you were doing? Getting her to leave town and leave him?" Nickol turned Nevina towards the living room, shoving her down on the cough and then sitting beside her, wrapping her as tight into his arms as he could.

"John seemed to think so. He also asked me about some photos. I don't know that I have anything that I shouldn't." Nevina sighed. "And that means I have to go over them."

"We'll go over them." Nickol's finger on her lips silenced her protest. "We'll go over them together. I've been over the photos that Geoff and I took and passed them on to who they needed to go to. Aidan is in charge of that investigation although he seems to think that it connects with the beaver family that I found." His head went down on hers. "I want this over, sweetheart. I want to live life with you and this is getting in the way."

Nevina slumped against him, exhausted from the emotions that had wracked her body that afternoon.

"I do too. I choose peace, Nickol. Peace that only God can give. We need to literally pray for that and choose that every day." She raised her head to study his profile, seeing his acceptance of her words.

"We do. And now that you're home, we'll spend time seeking that." Nickol looked down at her before he kissed her. "Emma has sent on some more material."

"Can we leave it for tonight or does she feel we need to go over it now?" Nevina hoped that they could leave it but she could tell from the look on Nickol's face that they wouldn't. "Okay, then. Let's eat and then spend time in prayer before we look at what there is." She wrapped a hand around his. "How did the others do it as this point? We don't have much of an idea as to who it is. Even the envelope that I was given didn't help much."

———

"No, it didn't." Nickol began to laugh. "Burnie sent on a logic puzzle outline for us. He says that they used it for some of their guys and it did work."

Nevina began to laugh at that, a much needed release. She knew Burnie and some of the wild ideas that he could come up with.

"Only Burnie. And we will look at that."

Neither of the couple made much of an effort to rise, instead bowing their heads before their Abba Father and spending time just waiting on Him and His leading. When they rose, there was peace in their hearts and a determination as well to solve their mystery and quickly.

Chapter 35

Nevina rose from her desk chair in the early morning hours the next day, stretching and then rubbing at the back of her neck. They had been working for hours on what had been provided, at times bickering amicably over their thoughts. Nickol had transferred Burnie's logic problem to a sheet of paper on the wall and they had both provided and removed names and information from it. Nevina walked over to study it, nodding. They were close, she felt, to knowing who it was. An arm around her drew her back against Nickol.

"Nickol? How are you feeling?" Nevina waited for him to speak, knowing that he would when he felt he could.

Nickol shrugged. He still hurt but the pain was fading. The bruises were turning yellow and green and healing. His wrist would heal. It was the mental and emotional trauma that he was having trouble dealing with. Darci had been in touch, prodding him to talk. He had been grateful for that.

"I'm getting there, I think, sweetheart." His chin rested on the top of her head. "What are your thoughts about this?"

"My thoughts? We need to take a break from this and get some sleep. We're not working in the morning, are we?"

"No, Erik told me not to come in. There have been men around the building, looking for me. He doesn't want to risk them finding me there." Nickol was frustrated at that.

"He's right. They would do that. Did he call in anyone?"

"He did. The last time they were there. He had them arrested for trespassing. From what he was told, they are wanted in many cities for crimes. They won't be back out." Nickol shrugged once more. "It's who is replacing them that we don't know."

Nevina hugged him and then walked away, heading for their bedroom. She stood for a moment, staring at the wall, not seeing the large framed photo of a favourite waterfall that hung above the bed. She sighed, thinking that she was doing that too much before she reached for her night clothes and headed for a shower. Rubbing at her wet hair, Nevina puzzled through what they had been reading. Something was missing and she knew that she would not sleep until she thought it through.

Nickol had seated himself once more at his desk, pulling the last few pages towards him. Emma had been sending him more information, almost more than he could handle. And Micah's Kat, who ran a family tree program, had provided information on suspects, as much as she felt that she could ethically do.

Nevina set a mug of coffee beside Nickol, not seeing him rouse from his reading, before she padded on bare feet to read the information on the sheets along the wall. Setting aside her own mug of coffee, Nevina reached for a marker and began to trace and number the information. That was not something that had been done, and she felt strongly that she needed to do that. She treated it as a photo that she was editing, picking apart the words, names, and occupations. She stepped back at last, frowning at her work before she felt a surge of fear through her. Turning, Nevina found Nickol watching her intently, his finger marking his place in his reading.

"What did you discover, sweetheart? And I know that you did." Nickol reached out a hand for her.

Nevina almost ran towards him to be swept close to his heart. She shuddered as she thought through the names that had come to her.

"I know who it is. And it's not who we thought. They are just outliers as they call them, sent in to muddle the mystery." She leaned back to look up at him, seeing the confidence that he had in her. She named the people, watching as he wrote each one down as she named them.

"Are these in particular order?" Nickol felt her nod against him. "From lowest to highest?" Again, he felt her nod. "Okay, we send them on to Emma and the others. For now, let's find our prayer corner. It's only going to get a lot worse." He hadn't had a chance to say anything to her but he had discovered that there had been men wandering around their home, trying to find a way in. They had not hidden their faces very well. He had copied the video feed and sent it on to John and Jerome. He had hesitated but sent it on to Erik as well, just so he would be prepared if the men showed up there looking for him.

"They are. I am afraid, Nickol. So deeply afraid. How do we live our lives right now, knowing that they are out there, waiting for an opportunity to kill us? And you need to show me that video that you don't want to. I hear sounds outside when I was changing." She leaned against him, not sure what more to say.

Nickol sighed. He hadn't hidden anything from her that he wanted to. Now, they had to make plans, and make plans they would. He just didn't know how well those plans would work.

"We need to plan, sweetheart. On our own for now. The guys will want to get involved, you know that, as will our families."

"I know." Nevina frowned for a moment. "How do we plan then to involve everyone and yet protect them while drawing out those people?" She stabbed a finger at the paper. "And we will need to draw them out. They're not going to walk right to us." She turned to look at him as he made a sound. "Nickol?"

"That's what we do. We plan to have them walk up to us. We'll have protection around us of course. Now, who all do we draw in?" Nickol sighed himself. "The bigger question is who do we not involve? Do you realize how many have reached out to us so far?"

"I know." Nevina began to laugh. "If this was a mystery novel, the author would be freaking out about now, having all those characters walk into the story. And we will use them. I just haven't figured it out yet." She stopped speaking for a moment before she spoke rapidly, coming up with a plan.

Nickol made notes, questioning her when he needed to, and then helping to refine her plans.

"Will this work?" Nevina was not sure if her plans would or not.

"I think it just might. It will take a few days to get this all organized. We need to reach out to our friends. I know everyone will want to be involved and we'll involve as many as we can." Nickol hugged her and then kissed her. "For now, we'll pray over it and wait for God's leading on it. We'll still move forward until and unless He stops us."

"I have peace about this, sweetheart." Nevina hugged Nickol, before she was on her feet, heading for the copier with the papers in hand to make copies. "We'll need to get these to the team leaders, Jerome and John, Erik, and whoever else needs them." She spun around, a smile on her face. "Did I tell you that Eddie and Ben are back in town? They're very eager to help end this for us."

"No, I didn't know that they were. And what's this I hear about John and Mary? He started to say something that last day they were here and stopped."

"He's resigned from the hospital. They are setting up a program or whatever you want to call it to come in and help others like they did for us. It's a calling, Mary said, that they have felt strongly about for years. I think it's wonderful."

"And it is. And now, do you know that it's time for us to be getting up?" Nickol laughed at the look on her face. "I know. We didn't sleep but we need to keep to our schedule as much as we can. I'll head off for the office with what I need to take there. You're going to be out and about in town with your camera."

"And I will be. I know that God will protect us but I'm still scared. We need to keep in earnest prayer over the next few days." Nevina walked away, heading for the bedroom to dress for the day. She stared down at the night clothes that she had donned after her shower and sighed. This was not how her life was to be.

Chapter 36

Later that day, John stared down at the papers that Nickol kept shoving at him before he looked up at his friend. He frowned at the look on Nickol's face. Something had changed and he didn't know what.

"What is this?" John scanned through them, seeing the orderly notes and numbered paragraphs.

"It's our plan to end this. We worked all night on it last night. We need this over, John, and soon. It's wearing Nevina down even though she won't say anything. She never complains about anything, as you know. And I want it over. I want to live life with my love and sweetheart and can't, fearing for her very life and for mine." Nickol walked away, nodding at Jerome and Edward as he passed them.

"John?" Jerome reached for the papers, reading through them, Edward at his shoulder. "Did they just do this?"

"Apparently. Last night, he said. I'm afraid for them, Jerome. How do we keep them safe?" John turned to his supervisor, surprised at the look on his face.

"It's not up to us, John. It's up to them. They are taking a step that they need to. They have included us as much as they can. We can't stop them unless it puts others at great risk. That's the unknown, isn't it? Keep in touch with them and work with them. For now, we each have to be somewhere else, don't we?" Jerome walked away, leaving Edward and John sharing a look before they took headed for the crime scenes that they needed to be at.

Nevina watched as Nickol slid behind the wheel of his truck, not questioning what was said. She had watched John's reaction and read correctly that he was upset with their plans.

"He didn't like our plans." Nevina reached for Nickol's hand.

"No, I don't know that he did, but he won't stop us. He has no legal recourse to do that." Nickol grinned at her. "For now, we're free of any responsibility such as work. It's Saturday. How be we go out for lunch and then wander through some of those stores you like?"

"We can do that. There's Nigel. Who's with him?" Nevina didn't recognize the lady.

"With Nigel? Elizabeth. She's a friend from years ago. She had left town but kept in touch with him. He had wanted to date her but she moved. It looks as if they're together. Want to double date?" He laughed as Nevina sprang from the truck and ran towards Nigel, hugging both him and the lady.

Late that afternoon, Nigel stood shoulder to shoulder with Nickol, laughing at the ladies. They were deep into a discussion, not watching the men at all.

"Nevina's good for Elizabeth. She's uncertain as to whether she should have come back to town." Nigel was deeply in love with her and had been for years. She had acknowledged that she loved him that very morning and that she had left town because she was afraid that he didn't love her.

"She is. She reaches out and down into people, bringing out their best. She's always been able to do that. Others see that as a fault. It's not. It's how God uses her." Nickol shivered in a sudden gust of wind. "How be head back to our place? We can grill something for a meal."

"Sounds like a plan." Nigel walked forward and wrapped Elizabeth in a hug, drawing her attention from Nevina. "It's okay, love. We're heading to Nickol's. He's invited us for a meal." He laughed at the look on Nevina's face. "Didn't tell you that?"

"No, he didn't, but it's okay. We have chicken that we were going on to grill and there's more than enough." Nevina frowned at them for a moment before her face cleared. "And we'll let you in on our plans." She walked away as Nigel opened his mouth to ask a question.

Nigel set aside the papers that he had been reading, knowing that he had to talk them over with his brother. He was just unsure how to do that and he never had a problem discussing anything with him.

"Nickol? You're sure about this?"

Nickol nodded, knowing that Nigel had picked up on.

"We are. We have to go on the offensive. Sitting at home, being on the defensive, hasn't worked.

They're watching us too closely. We're not getting the threats that are normally seen."

"We wondered about that." Nigel nodded, having discussed that with their father and Trevor. "When?"

"In the next two days. We need to bring others in on the planning. We've arranged a conference call with them all tomorrow night. If you could be here?" Nickol was suddenly unsure about having his brother involved.

"We'll be here. Elizabeth and I. Mom and Dad. Trevor and Ruth. Eddie and Ben are still in town." Nigel grinned at Nevina as she sat next to Nickol. "We have almost too many people."

"We do. That's why we work in shifts with them. Breck was working on that, he said, with the guys from the Foundation. Anna has called. She wants to be in on this as well. She regrets that her nephew appears to have been involved in crime with some of those we suspect. And no, we didn't give her any names. She provided them to us." Nevina was saddened as well. She had spent a lot of time just speaking and praying with Anna, helping that lady to see that she was not at fault. It would take a lot of counselling for Anna to overcome what she had lived with for years.

"So we plan tomorrow night. It's going to take some time to organize everything." Nigel looked at Nickol and Nevina as they laughed at him. "It is."

"Not really. The planning is being done even as we speak. We have many friends involved in this who have been through adventures. You know that, Nigel. And they are using the experiences that they had to help with us and to plan to keep us safe. No amount of planning will keep us totally safe but we will do what we can.”

“John? Is he involved?” Elizabeth’s quiet voice and question drew their attention to her.

“As much as he can be. We can’t totally involve him as he is a police officer but he has a copy of what you’ve just read.” Nickol sighed, something he seemed to be doing a lot of. “For now, we need to pray and pray long and hard. It will be God who keeps us safe and protects us.” He shared a look with Nevina. “We have peace about this, Nigel. We are choosing peace in this. We are scared, yes, and worried. But God has promised to give us peace. If one of us doesn’t make it, we have reassured one another that it is in God’s will for us.”

Nigel nodded, knowing to some extent how his brother thought. His own arm tightened around his lady, knowing that he wouldn’t be at that place where Nickol and Nevina were.

Chapter 37

Nevina rubbed her hands along her jeans legs the next night. She was nervous, to say the least, at what Nickol had described as crunch time. Her home felt full of people and computers as others were signing in to a program that would allow them all to meet. Elizabeth's hand rested on hers for a moment, just letting Nevina know that she was not alone.

"What happens now, Nevina? Are you sure about this?" Elizabeth's quiet question steeled Nevina's resolve.

"We go over our plans. Any changes will be discussed and agreed on. We have four team leaders with loads of experience in keeping people alive. We have people officers on here who are friends. Everyone of them has faced an adventure themselves and with their friends. Darci will give us a more detailed profile. From what I understand, she is always bang on with her assessment." Nevina sighed. "I want this over, Elizabeth and over now."

"And it will be. God is here, Nevina. He has never left you or forsaken you." Elizabeth's head bowed as she prayed for her friend.

Nigel was watching the two ladies from where he was seated beside Ben.

"Ben? Will this work?"

"I don't see why it won't. We went through this with my son and my niece, to say nothing of others we know. Frankie and Deirdre joke about how scary she can be but trust me, she was afraid. When Timothy went through what he did and disappeared on us, both Marg and I feared that we would not see him again. But God protected him and Rachel. Now, He's protecting your brother and his bride. You may not like what they face and they won't either but it is what God has chosen for them."

"I know." Nigel looked around as silence began to fill the room. "It's time for our prayers isn't it?"

"It is. And those are what we need to finalize our plans and then implement them safely." Ben's head bowed as they began their time of prayer, knowing full well that it was only God who would keep this couple safe.

Conversation was spiced with laughter and good-natured teasing even as the plans were discussed and refined. The four team leaders were impressed with the plans and said so. Nevina had blushed at their praise, not realizing that she had led Nickol in planning a well-thought out plot to save themselves. Nickol had been quick to credit her with the major plans.

Locking up after the ones in their home had gone their way, Nickol paused for a moment, his head dropping in fatigue. He was still trying to recover from his beating, a beating and chilling from the damp cold earth that could have killed him. The doctors had been frank with him, answering any and all questions that he had. He had not told Nevina that he had sought out those answers but he didn't think that he had to. She seemed to know when he had spoken with the medical personnel.

Nevina walked into his hug, her arms around him as she hugged him back. This was a dangerous time for them, they knew, waiting to put their plan into play. They were trusting in their friends to help protect them but circumstances could change those very plans. They didn't expect to leave their home over the next couple of days, working from home as they could. Two days was what they had decided would be the time frame from that meeting to when they were out there, openly searching for the man responsible. That man was still in town, trying his best to hide, but there were people watching them, people not in on the plans but who wanted it over for Nickol and Nevina.

Two mornings later, Nevina roused, finding herself tucked tight to Nickol's side, his arm around her holding her close. He was still asleep, she knew, listening to the sounds of his deep breathing. Today was the day, she knew, that they had decided to put their plans into placc. Thcir fricnds would be there, taking time out of their own lives to watch and protect. They had planned as much as they could. They just couldn't plan for the unexpected. Abe, Don, and Richard had all warned them about that, Peter nodding in agreement. John and Jerome had been around, not saying much, but listening to them. Off-duty officers would be around as well, Jerome had been adamant about that. Nevina had begun to laugh, drawing frowns from the men until she stated that there was no way that they could hide themselves, not with the contingent that would be following or waiting for them. The men had shaken their heads even as they had laughed at her nonsense.

Rising from the bed, Nevina turned for a moment to study Nickol. Her love for him had grown day by day and they never failed to tell one another of that love. She was grateful for the man he had become, fulfilling the promise of his youth. Nevina walked away, finding the clothes that had been laid out the night before and dressing before she headed for the kitchen. Turning on only a low light, she squinted at the clock noting that it was only four in the morning. She would not sleep any more. Instead, Nevina reached to turn on the coffee pot and then with a full mug in hand, headed for her prayer corner, to spend time in prayer.

Nickol was on his feet an hour later, looking for Nevina. He reached for a fresh mug of coffee for her and then one for himself, setting them on the table beside her and sweeping her into his arms.

"Couldn't sleep?" His voice was low and hesitant, not at all his normal strong vibrant tones.

"I could. I just had enough sleep." Nevina tilted her head to look at him. "I didn't wake you, did I?"

"No, God did. We need to spend this time in prayer. I don't think either of us feel much like eating." His voice was sober as was his face, matching Nevina's.

"We do. Abe called earlier, just to pray with me. He said not to wake you up." Nevina yawned, her thoughts distracted for a moment. "What can we do to repay them?"

"They won't want that, you know, but we'll think of something." Nickol's eyes closed as he began to pray, asking for peace in what they were facing.

Nevina's voice picked up his words, asking for peace but also for confidence in their plans. She also asked that if the plans were contrary to God's will, that He stop them. For now, she hadn't gotten the sense that they needed to do just that.

Chapter 38

Hand in hand, Nickol and Nevina walked towards the well-worn path of the forest near where it had all started. They had hesitated at first, not sure that their plans were correct and then had moved forward, confident that they were taking the right step. Friends were around them and along the pathway, hidden from view but ready to step in when needed. They knew that there were some with video cameras to capture the moment of confrontation, and confrontation it would be. Neither one was totally clear as to why they had bene targeted but they knew that would come and come shortly.

Nevina paused as she reached the edge of a clearing. This is it, she thought. This is where we meet our enemy. Only, we don't know why he's an enemy.

Nickol's hand tightened on hers as he too paused, his eyes searching the area. He could feel the evil around them, knowing that this is where they made their stand. He had caught a glimpse of Abe, Richard, Don, and Peter, just quick enough for him to know that they were there and had men surrounding them. This was on purpose, he decided, knowing that the reassurance of them there would give them the strength to go ahead with what was needed.

"All set, sweetheart?" Nickol's voice was kept low. He made no movement to walk forward, waiting for Nevina to indicate that she was ready to go.

"I don't know that I am, Nickol, but we need to, don't we? How did they all do this? I'm terrified, you know." Nevina's voice wobbled as she spoke, betraying her nerves and fear.

"I am too, sweetheart. `I am so afraid that I will lose you." Nickol breathed out a prayer before he stiffened himself and then stepped forward, Nevina's hand tight in his.

Nevina looked around, sensing danger approaching them before her feet reluctantly stopped. He was here, twenty feet in front of them. She had not seen him appear but he had.

"Nevina?" Nickol looked down at her, questioning why she had stopped.

"He's here, Nickol. In front of us. How did he get here?" Nevina was puzzling that even as the man stood and glared at them, a weapon held in his hand and dangling at his side.

"He's armed, sweetheart. That we figured he would be." Nickol made no movement to to walk forward even as he was ordered to. "Not happening, Gray. We're not moving towards you."

"You will." Carl Gray walked towards them, the weapon now raised. "You're going to do what I say or she dies."

"I don't think so, Gray." Nickol's voice rang out with confidence. "We're not your captives. Not yet, any way. So how be you explain yourself?" Nickol saw men moving in behind Gray and saw other men being led away in handcuffs. He felt Nevina's hand tighten on his. They needed to keep Gray's attention on them and not what was happening behind him.

"You will be. I have it all planned out. You're going to work for me, Nickol, and find me the animals that I need. Your wife?" Gray flicked a finger. "I really don't care what happens to her. She's not going with us. You're the one that I need."

Nickol's face darkened with anger, having a good sense of what Gray was meaning. Nevina would not walk away from there if Gray had his way.

"Tell me, Gray. How did you get involved in this poaching?" Nickol was desperate to keep the man talking. "And why choose me?"

"My uncle got me involved when I was a teenager. He poached the animals for what he needed from them. You know what I mean. And then when he died, I just took over. It's too bad he had to die so young." Gray sneered at them. "I can tell you. You won't be telling anyone else. I killed him when I was seventeen. He was getting old and senile and wanting to get out of the business. It's too lucrative to do that." His weapon pointed at them once more. "And you will come with me."

"First, tell me. Why me? I did nothing to you." Nickol was genuinely puzzled at that. He looked down at Nevina for a moment as she whispered something.

"Your sister." Nevina's voice rang out in confidence. "She wanted to be with Nickol, deciding that he would be her boyfriend and then marry her. Only, he never looked her way. No one did. She was an outcast, just because of how she acted. She was never liked. She tried too hard to fit in but her coarseness and brazenness made it impossible." Nevina was sure on her words. She had not considered that before but hearing Gray speak, she knew it was the truth. "You fixated on Nickol, thinking that he would be the one to bring her to the right side of town as we say. Only, he never looked her way. He had no reason to be around her. None of our friends did. And you resented that. You blamed everyone else except your sister. Did you kill her too?" The look on Gray's face gave them the answer that they needed. He had in fact killed his sister, having made it look like a suicide.

John stood behind Gray, his face blank but his mind racing. The teams had been looking into him over the last couple of days and that fact had been raised. Her death was being once more investigated, the first investigation shoddy at best. Jerome had been muttering that someone must have been paid off.

Gray's face darkened at he once more raised his weapon. The couple could see the anger and venom on his face. Nickol gave a shout and wrapped Nevina in his arms, throwing them sideways into the long grass and then shoving her forward at a rapid crawl away from the area. Hands reached to raise them to their feet and run them away to safety. Afterwards, neither Nickol or Nevina could say who it had been and none of the men would admit to it. It was just who they were and what they did.

John and Edward flung themselves at Gray, taking him to the ground. They struggled to control him. Edward with his arms wrapped around Gray's torso. John had his hands around Gray's, squeezing at the wrist and shaking the hand until the weapon was dropped. An officer moved in to prevent Gray from reaching for it. Still struggling as his hands were cuffed behind him, Gray's voice spews vile curses at them.

John stood, breathing hard as he looked around. Abe nodded at him. John breathed a sigh of relief. Nickol and Nevina were finally safe. They had to finish off the investigation and draw up the charges but Gray would be in jail. He was the only one who remained at large.

"We're done, Abe. Thanks to you, Don, Richard, and Peter, Nickol and Nevina are safe." John reached to shake the men's hands.

"God protected them, John. We were just His hands and feet on earth." Richard walked away, his emotions in a turmoil for a moment. It had been close, he knew, too close.

John walked off after the other officers, Edward pacing bedside him. Neither man spoke but they didn't have to. God had prevailed once more and that was all they could say.

Chapter 39

Three days later, Nickol turned as he felt a hand on his shoulder. His father simply hugged his son, grateful that their adventure was now over. He stood back with his hands resting on Nickol's shoulder before he tapped them and walked away, his emotions overcoming him for a moment.

Nickol watched his father walk away before he felt another arm across his shoulders. Trevor stood there, watching the young man that he had watched grow from a child. He could ask for no one else for his beloved daughter. He knew that Nevina had always had feelings for Nickol but would never have said anything.

"Trevor?" Nickol's voice held a question.

"It's okay, Nickol. You and Nevina are safe. God protected you from more danger than we even realized."

"He did. I didn't know that Gray was involved in more than just poaching. He was a danger to everyone here."

It had come out in the investigation that Gray had been a murderer for hire as well as a poacher. Numerous investigations were now underway in their town and in surrounding towns, murders that had never been solved. It was felt that he would be the one involved and would be facing many years in jail. He had been behind everything almost that Nickol and Nevina had faced, other than their marriage. Gray had denied that, spewing venom at the officer who was questioning him.

Nevina looked around the living room at their family gathered there. Peter and his wife and his team and their wives as well as John, Edward, Jerome, Slavin and Shaye, and Roane and Ragen had all gathered there that Sunday afternoon, just to wind down from the investigation. John wouldn't say much, other than what he had. That was okay with them.

Nigel approached his brother late that afternoon. They had found themselves outside in the yard, most of everyone else having left.

"Nickol? Are you okay now?" Nigel waited patiently for Nickol to respond.

"I'm not sure, Nigel. I am really not. It's going to take a while for it all to sink in as to why and who. And Nevina is struggling with that as well." Nickol tilted his head back and looked up. "Erik told me to take next week, just to get my head straight again. I shouldn't but I will. Nevina and I are going to head away for a few days, find somewhere that we're on our own and talk. We need to do that. This was so rushed on us." Nickol was sober as he spoke, knowing that the couple needed to talk but not sure that they could.

"You do need that. You're her heart, Nickol. You always have been. Just as she's yours." Nigel grinned at his brother. "Would you have ever asked her out on a date?"

Nickol shrugged, his eyes narrowing as he watched his brother.

"You wouldn't have." His voice held an accusation.

"Wouldn't have what?" Nigel continued to grin at his brother, knowing full well what he was asking.

"You wouldn't have set us up on a date." Nickol's eyes closed for a moment. "That's exactly what you would have done."

"I might have. If you hadn't asked her out, I likely would have. You needed some help there, brother." Nigel's arm came around his brother's shoulders. "I love you, Nickol. I hated what you had to go through but you have come through with a peace from God that not many of us get."

"You're right. He did give us that." Nickol was sober as he spoke. "Nevina prayed that way. I thought it strange at first until she told me that all we needed to do was ask for His peace and it was already ours. When she explained it that way, how could I not?"

"She's a wise lady. Always has been. Her friendship is one that Elizabeth and I cherish. We're taking off now. We're heading out for dinner." Nigel reached to hug his brother, walking away from him. He found Nevina and hugged her as well before the door closed behind him.

Nevina stared at the door and then turned to find Nickol. He was still standing where Nigel had left him, lost in thought.

"Nickol? What was with Nigel?" Nevina walked into Nickol's hug and his kiss.

"Nigel? He told me that you had always been a wise lady." Nickol looked down at her upturned face. "And he's correct. You always have been. You see deeper into people and things than the rest of us do. Don't ever change."

"I don't intend to. Don't sell yourself short. You read situations better than anyone else I know." Nevina leaned against in, relishing the strength that she was held with. "What now, Nickol?"

"What now? Next week, we find that cabin in the woods and spend some time with you and me. And we talk. Not just about what we went through but our plans and dreams. We've talked about them before as individuals. Now we can to talk about what we want as a couple." He grinned at her. "I like that thought."

"So do I." Nevina shoved away from him, pacing the yard, knowing that he was turning in his spot to follow her path. "Nickol? What about a family? We never spoke about that."

"We really haven't had a chance to talk about things, have we? Are you trying to tell me something?" Nickol walked rapidly towards her, sweeping her into another hug.

"No. It's just that's something we have to consider, whether we want a family or pets or whatever."

"Pets? Do you have something in mind?" Nickol had reached for the little calico kitten, who was growing up far too fast and had entwined herself into their lives and hearts.

Nevina shook her head. She was just throwing words out there, she decided, nervous to be alone with Nickol without danger hanging over their heads.

"No. But we may want to consider that as well. Nigel was dropping hints about a calico kitten that he found."

Nickol began to laugh, hugging Nevina tighter.

"He'll never give her up, you do know that? I hope you didn't agree to take her."

Nevina smirked at him.

"I said no. Would have served him right if I had said yes." Their laughter rang out through the yard, bringing a lightness to their hearts that was so sorely needed.

Epilogue

Seven months later, Nevina stared at her reflection in the full-length mirror hanging behind the bedroom door. She smoothed the skirt of the flowered dress she wore, not sure that she was dressed appropriately. Nickol had asked her to dress up, that he wanted to take her somewhere special for the day.

Nickol waited somewhat impatiently for Nevina to appear. He was in dress slacks, dress shirt and tie, the day being somewhat warm. He turned the box over and over in his hands, not seeing as Nevina hesitated before walking up to him and into his hug. His love for her had grown day by day. She challenged him in a good way but brought a spice to his life that was refreshing, finding humour in the unexpected.

"Nickol? We don't have to go anywhere." Nevina was not sure still what he was up to.

"We do. First." He opened the box to reveal a beautiful gold locket that he fastened around her neck. "I saw this and had to get it for you. You deserve so much."

Nevina was shaking her head at him. He was always bringing her something, even if it was just her favourite chocolate bar or a bouquet of flowers.

"You give me so much, Nickol." She reached to kiss him. "Now, where are we off to?"

"Barnabas asked if we could come for the day. They've prepared a thank you on our behalf for everyone who was involved. He said his Dad and the board met about a month ago and asked that they do this." Nickol was not sure how Nevina would take that.

"They did? They are so wonderful, being the hands and feet of God on earth." Nevina bit at her lip, a sign that she was uncertain. "It's all day?"

"For as long as we want. I know that's not what you expected. I couldn't say no. We wanted to do something."

"You do realize how many people there are? And their children?" At his nod, Nevina's face went against his chest. "Too many." She looked up at him. "We need to talk, Nickol."

"We will. Let's get through the day and then we will." Nickol locked the door behind them and then seated her into his truck, driving away without any worry that they were in danger.

Early that evening, Nevina kicked off her sandals near the front door and padded through the house in her bare feet. She was tired, but it was a good tired, she decided. It had been a long day but one that was so needed. Trying to thank everyone had been exhausting but the Barnabas Foundation had gone well beyond what she had expected in their planning and presentation.

Nickol stood for a moment and watched his lady, his hand loosening his tie before he pulled it off and tossed it to the kitchen table. Nevina was lost in another world, he decided, and it wasn't just from today. To have been asked to head up a wilderness foundation charity for the Foundation had not been what either one had expected. They had been given the information and told to pray over it for as long as it took. That was how that board worked. They prayed about a new charity. Then they prayed for a couple and when the board met to discuss the couple, that couple was always an unanimous choice. If the couple refused, then the board continued to pray.

"I wasn't expecting that job offer." Nickol wrapped Nevina close to him as they sat on the couch.

"I wasn't either. But we're both restless right now in our work. We'll pray it over but I suspect that we'll take it on." Nevina leaned against him.

"I agree." Nickol dropped a kiss on the top of her head. "But that's not what's bothering you."

'No, it's not." Nevina rubbed her hands together. "When we talked months ago about a family, I don't know that we ever really decided if we wanted one."

Nickol watched her face, seeing her hesitation to speak with him but also seeing the news that she was struggling to tell him.

"We're going to be parents?" At her nod, he kissed her. "I'm glad. You'll make a wonderful mother. And this new line of work is better suited for you."

Nevina poked him, a smile fleeting across her face.

"You'll be the father and head of the house in God's sight that we need. It's not for a few months yet, so we have time to plan. I just don't want to tell anyone yet."

"We don't have to." Nickol's head bowed as he prayed for their family and for the little one who would join them. He sat back at last, the love of his life in his arms. He gave a gentle smile as she slept. His thoughts turned to prayer once more, thanking God for never leaving them, for bringing them through the adventure, and then blessing them with a family on the way. He knew that he could only go on with God's help. The peace that God gave was growing in both of them more and more. They had chosen peace over worry and anger. God was blessing that choice.

Thank you for joining the adventures of Nickol and Nevina in Book Three of In His Choosing, Choosing Peace. The story never writes as I envision it but it is always how God has chosen the words for me.

Nickol and Nevina could have chosen so many different emotions and thoughts. Instead, they chose peace and prayed for that. How many times have we chosen peace? For myself, it's not something that I would normally desire but now? That has changed. He has promised us peace, not as the world gives it, but as He alone gives it.

Now, the unruly characters that can't stay out of anyone's adventures. This time? There were many who became involved. Friends from Oak City, Riverville, Mistletoe, Elmton all had to join in. Without them, I don't know that the story would have moved along as it did. I always enjoy bringing in some characters. This time? They just kept dragging in more and more. I lost count of how many when you consider the men and ladies and their spouses. And then their children.

Now, as to my writing. For now, I am stepping back from it. Disability issues are increasing and making it tough to write. On the other hand, I found out recently that thirty-six of my books were pirated and used for AI training, without my permission, knowledge or compensation. That has dug deep into my dreams of writing. I pour my heart and soul into my novels and this has really stung. For now, I have taken down my website. Most of my books will no longer be available to the public. If there is a book that you wish to reach, please contact me (rmbacon58@gmail.com) and I will gladly get one to you.

God bless each one of you as you journey through life. He will never leave you, never forsake you, never ask you to go where He has not already gone. In this series, they have chosen life, joy, and peace. May you do the same, finding God answering your prayers for these.

Ronna